KISSES AREN'T ALWAYS SWEET

KISSES AREN'T ALWAYS SWEET

JDANIELS

sepia™

KISSES AREN'T ALWAYS SWEET

ISBN-13: 978-1-58314-692-7
ISBN-10:   1-58314-692-X

www.kimanipress.com

Printed in U.S.A.

This book is dedicated to all the women who have gone through pain and betrayal in a twisted society. A society where love is never what it used to be, and where cheating has a new face.

And to all the men out there, be careful where you lay your head. It's a thin line between love and hate. And kisses aren't always sweet.

JD*

ACKNOWLEDGMENTS

There are so many people that I want to thank for the development of this project. First of all, my editor, Glenda Howard: Thank you for your patience and endurance and continuous belief in me and my work. I know I gave you a hard time, but your empathy and professionalism motivated me to get off my behind. I love working with you. I promise I'll be good next time around! To Linda Gill, General Manager of Sepia Books. I love that you love what I write. I hope we have a long working relationship together. To the Harlequin family: I am excited and look forward to this new stage in publishing, and I am so thrilled to be a part of your new line. My agent, Sara Camilli: Sara, it's been a wonderful experience having you representing me all these years. It's always so easy to talk to you and have you champion me and my endeavors. Here's to many years and novels to come!

To my family who pushed me and encouraged me and are always ready to read my next book. Thank you for never giving up on me, even when things get rough.

V. Anthony Rivers: you are a brother to me and I love you so much. Congratulations for all the great things that are happening in your writing career. I can't wait until we make literary magic together.

Darrin Lee: your fantastic drive pushes me forward, and your encouraging chats make me move a little bit faster.

I want to mention by name some strong women who encourage me: Dianna, Ny-Tina, Angel, my sister who drove me up the wall to hurry up and finish this book! Desiney, Mary, the drill sergeant, or so they say. But you aren't that tough to me, lol.

Special love to the Wal-Mart Family. Who's number one? You are!

And last but not least. Thank you to my loyal fans who even after two years since my last release, still pick up and buy anything I write. I promise I won't take so long next time around. I hope you love this one.☺

PROLOGUE

She knew the makeup of men almost better than she knew her own. She knew what made them tick, and she used it to her advantage. Most men were crafty and conniving liars, especially *him.*

She sighed at his memory and blocked him from her mind. She had better things to do than think of the dead. *May he rest in hell,* she thought. She licked her lips, then casually signed on to the internet.

You got mail! the opening screen cried out.

She smiled while clicking the little blue mailbox with the yellow envelope peeking out. She had two e-mails waiting for her, both from the same person: BmoreLova.

Wassup, gorgeous? I can't seem to get you out of my mind. I can't wait till this evening. I'm gonna make that body sing, ya heard me? Holla back at me when you get this.

She laughed to herself. *Yeah, I bet you can't wait,* she thought. She clicked on e-mail number two.

I haven't heard from you yet, beautiful. I still don't understand why you won't give me your cell phone number. But that's okay. You are one mysterious woman. I'll see you at 9:30, in front of the convention center. BE THERE!

Looking down at her watch, she noticed the time. It was already 9:00 p.m. That gave her thirty minutes to beat the Baltimore traffic and have her first face-to-face with BmoreLova. It had been a month, corresponding with BmoreLova. He thought he knew her. At least as well as she would allow him to get to know her, via online.

By now it was 9:20 and she wheeled her rented dark blue Jeep Liberty past the Inner Harbor, heading for West Pratt Street. Although she drove as if in a hurry, she didn't really have to. That Negro would be there, she knew that much. Men never turned down sexual opportunities. Her stomach had stayed cramped the whole month she spent talking to BmoreLova on the Internet. For every flirt, every cyberkiss, every sex session, and what BmoreLova thought was mutual masturbation, she was thinking about what she was going to do to him, what she was going to give him. She was doing it for her sisters; she was doing it for herself. She was doing it for the pain that was given to them, and the heartfelt torture that had destroyed her soul. She was the Robin Hood of womanhood. She was doing it for them, for herself... It was a kiss. It was a kiss, for every man who broke her heart.

That heart sped up, chilled, and grew cold as she got closer to her destination. She saw him and didn't have to wonder if she had the right man. He had described himself to a tee, and he looked just like his picture. Tall, light-skinned black man, with short dreadlocks and the beginnings of a goatee. He was leaning against the glass wall on the front side of the building. He looked excited.

She smirked. She would make their first meeting memorable for him. She pulled up at the curb and lowered the passenger-side window.

"Well, hello there," she said to him, smiling as she caught his eye. He couldn't see hers, though, since she had dark glasses on.

"Wassup, boo?" He leaned into the open window. "Can I hop inside?"

She nodded, looking at him mischievously.

Once he was inside, BmoreLova looked her up and down as she pulled away from the convention center. His eyes stopped when they reached her full, moist lips.

"You look just as good as your pictures," he noted. "Are you going to tell me your name now or do I still call you…"

"Jami, call me Jami." She reached over to him and licked his cheek like a cat slurping milk. "Meow," she cooed.

BmoreLova gave a slight feigned shiver. "Jami. I like that. Damn, girl, you know how to heat a nigga up. So what you gonna do with me? Are we going to your place?"

"Nope."

"So is it a big secret or something?"

"Didn't you tell me online that you love a touch of mystery?" she reminded him. "Trust me, you are never going to have another night like this one."

BmoreLova slid closer to the lady he called Jami and

began to rub her thigh, pushing her miniskirt upward. She laughed again and then pushed his hand away.

"Hold up. I can't drive while you're doing that. I'm gonna stop somewhere." She gave him a coy look.

"Are we going to your place?" he repeated. She shook her head at his question. "A hotel?" She shook her head again.

She wasn't heading to a hotel. She had a perfect spot picked out for their *quickie*. Only five minutes from the convention center was a back-alley entrance to Marshall's Crab Shack. BmoreLova frowned as they got to the shack, his nose turned up at the smell.

"You mean to tell me you wanna chill here?" he asked, amazed.

She gave him an innocent look, shrugged her shoulders, and turned the engine off. "We don't have to worry about being disturbed." She reached over, rubbing her long French-manicured nails over his cheek. What followed were her lips. BmoreLova moaned at the feel of her.

"You sure you don't want to go somewhere more comfortable to do this?" he asked.

"Let's get in the back."

BmoreLova looked around when she was quiet after that. He was waiting for her to say something else.

"The backseat of the car," she explained, giggling.

She ran her fingernail up the length of his manhood, threw him an air kiss, and then got in the back of the car, lounging against the leather seat.

As weird as her actions seemed, she knew BmoreLova

was turned on by the mystery of her. She had been like that since he'd first met her online. First it was her not wanting to send him a picture, which she later relented on, and then it was her no-phone-calls rule. He had told her once that he was almost sure she was married, probably with three kids and a dog, living some urban American dream. He had told her that he was what she needed to bring excitement to her life and to curtail the lonely episodes. Apparently he thought he was the answer to all that.

BmoreLova was laid out in the backseat and waiting for her next move. She slid over to him and hiked up her skirt. She wore no panties and her sex was shaved. Bmore-Lova looked down with his tongue almost hanging out of his mouth.

"Baby, get over here and let me get at that," he whispered.

She moved quickly over him. He didn't have to ask more than once. She grabbed him, wrapping her legs around his hips and jumping in his lap in one swift movement. She covered his mouth with hers and started tonguing him down, not giving him a chance to say another word, grinding herself against his bulge. He moaned as she indulged her hips, moving in an up-and-down fashion.

"Yeah, girl," he said in a pant. He reached under her skirt and cupped her ass. "Let me get my jeans loose. Hold up."

She paid him no attention but instead worked her lips down the base of his neck, nipping at his skin. This drew another muffled moan from him. She could tell he was getting a little too happy. She bit into his neck once more at the same time she secretly maneuvered the sharp, silvery instrument from her sleeve. She rubbed her fingers at the base of his neck, and just as BmoreLova whispered out some heated expression, she stabbed him there with her hypodermic needle, emptying the poison into him. He jumped at the needle prick and pulled back from her.

"What the hell... What the hell are you do—"

He didn't get to finish his sentence. His eyes rolled back into his head and right on cue, his heartbeat stopped. His body fell heavily against her and she shoved him off her, opening the door and pushing him to the ground.

She looked down at him. His eyes were open still because of the quickness with which the poison had invaded his system. She stooped down in front of him.

"Didn't you know?" she whispered. "Didn't you know you'd have to pay someday? Didn't you know you can't keep treating us like shit?"

Her heart was beating in a rush as she spoke. She paused and took a deep breath, then kissed her fingers and closed each of his eyes lovingly. She got up, got into her car, and pulled off.

Her job was done, at least for this night.

CHAPTER 1

Kimberla

I was on high alert. My heart was beating really fast, and it felt like I was sweating on the inside. I was seriously stressed and felt like I was losing my damn mind, but I was doing my best to cover it up with my tough-girl act. I took my time peeling the tender, young red potatoes that were going to be a staple part of my beef stew; yet still my nerves were racing. The sound of a feline roar startled me, and I quickly turned around. My sudden move made me miss the potato I was peeling and I ended up skinning my finger instead.

"Damn you, Jacob!" I cried out loud.

I rushed to the sink. My finger began steadily seeping blood. There was nothing more painful than a skinned finger. I could only imagine what it felt like to be scalped by Indians.

I moaned. "Damn, this hurts!" Pouting, I looked down at the gash and then applied pressure to stop the bleeding.

I could whine like a sissy at times but only when I was alone. I prided myself on being a strong woman, and lived by the creed "never let them see you sweat."

Sweating made me think of Jacob, a fellow FBI agent I'd been seeing. I loved the way he made me feel. God, I missed him. It wasn't just his sexy and oh-so-fine body, or the way he loved me down with it, bringing every fiber of my being alive and tingling...mmmm. No, I admired and respected his mind, too. I had a soft spot for Jacob, which was why this fat, fluffy beast he lovingly called Blu was in my place. Blu was his baby. Actually it had been his late wife's cat, and was a rather old animal. When he was away on assignment, as he was now, he always got someone to babysit for him. And me being the person that he said he trusted the most right now, I was perfect to keep an eye on his um...baby. Forget the fact that I absolutely abhorred animals, especially cats. But of course I couldn't say no. I agreed to cat-sit.

The cat did remind me of Jacob. I figured the least I could do was grin and bear it. For the past six weeks Jacob had been in Chicago helping to solve some drug-related string of murders, lending the expertise, the bureau felt, he'd gotten battling the underground war on crime.

I missed him desperately. Ever since our last case with Michael Riley had been solved, we'd spent every waking hour together. Our relationship had grown into something I never really believed existed: love. Or was it love? Jacob had said he loved me many times, and I melted at his words and the sincere look in his eyes. But I felt something else, too. Fear, I guess. I was not quite sure what it was yet, what the problem was, but my lips wouldn't allow the words "I love you, too," to go past them. Not quite yet. I knew my hesitancy hurt him, especially when he was so free with his own words of love. But in a way it felt like his constant pushing made me push back in the opposite direction. Like what in the hell did he want from me? Why couldn't it be enough that we were together? Why did men always have to put their stamp on a woman? Lay claim on us? That beast mentality is a bit much at times. I guess I'm too much of a woman to allow it to control me. At least that's what I tell myself.

I sighed, mumbling to myself. Even with all my brave talk, *I still missed him....*

"Oh, shit!" I almost bit my lip when I felt something hairy running across my feet. That damn Blu!

"Okay, damnit! That's the last straw!"

I had marched over to the kitchen closet to grab my broom, ready to make cat soup out of the beast, when my phone rang.

"You are literally saved by the bell, Blu," I whispered. "Hello?" I heaved into the phone, breathing deeply.

"How is my favorite agent today?" It was Agent Kyte Williams.

"Frustrated!"

"What's wrong?" Kyte laughed at my tone.

"Oh, nothing." I sighed. "What do you need? What's up?"

"Why does there have to be something up for me to call you?"

"Kyte, don't play with me. It's a Sunday and my caller ID says that you're at the office, so I know this isn't a social call. So again, what do you need?"

"Okay, okay. You got me." He paused, then mumbled to someone on the other end.

"Are you there?"

"Um…yes. Listen, Kimberla, I need you to come in for a while. I need to talk to you about something that's been developing. But I don't want to talk about it on the phone."

"Oh no, you don't!" I shouted. "For one, this is a Sunday and it's my day off. Two, I just started my dinner. And three, I have company coming over!"

Kyte was laughing in my ear. What was funny to him wasn't at all to me. I knew him so well. "And I can give you just one simple sentence that will knock all your objections out of the water. You, my dear Chameleon, are an FBI agent. There is no such thing as a day off."

I bit my lip. I hesitated to ask him but still spilled out the question of the century that had been plaguing my mind. "Have you heard anything new about my case?"

"Kimberla, you know they will get to it when they can. I thought we agreed not to focus on your reinstatement right now."

"Fine," I said, swallowing my disappointment.

"Patience, dear. Like I've told you before, you are lucky that all they did was demote you. I've known agents who were fired for less."

Did I really need to hear all that? Nope. I had known what would happen from the start. I had known the risk I was taking when I decided to take on Michael Riley, David Huggins, and the whole Mackings establishment. There is always recompense for our actions. You reap what you sow. My mom always told me that so I was ready for the repercussions. I owed it to Margo, my best friend and fellow agent, to do all I could to find her killer, and with Jacob's help, I did. I really didn't regret a thing. It was just hard sometimes. I had worked so hard to get where I was. I was born to be a leader, a special agent in charge. Now I was just plain old agent again.

"Kimberla, are you still there?" Kyte called out. "Don't get an attitude with me. I need you to get here as soon as possible."

"I don't have an attitude, Kyte."

"So are you coming?"

"Do I have a choice?"

I could almost feel Kyte smiling like the devil over the phone. I hung up in his face.

This was turning out to be not my day, at all! Not only had Kyte invaded my beef stew-time, but now I was stuck in godforsaken Silver Spring traffic trying to make it into D.C. The defroster was acting up in my car and the cloudy moisture in the air wasn't making it easy to keep clear windows. All I needed to complete the Friday the thirteenth spirit that had crept into my day was to see a black cat running across the street. Yeah, that would send my mood down the toilet, permanently.

I waited in traffic, tapping my foot impatiently, and then decided that instead of sitting around trippin' about fog and car malfunctions, I would give Kendra a call. Kendra was my girl, and one of my very best friends. Both of us had busy careers. We had grown up together, been best friends throughout high school, and had even gone to college together and had been roommates. During that time she was one of the few females that didn't make me feel insecure, or that didn't act like I was a he-man because I preferred the comfort of jeans and sneakers over dresses and high heels. But after graduation, while I was off chasing criminals and racing my way up the ladder of success, Kendra had been off at medical school. She was now Dr. Kendra Gray, a renowned and very successful neurologist at John Hopkins Hospital. In reality, my friends were few and far between, but I made a point of staying in touch with the few I did have, no matter the years or changes in life. To me, friendship is something to be nurtured, the way you nurture a baby, or water a plant. If you don't feed it, it dies. I had three true friends in my life: Margo Hunter, my godsister, Sharon, and of course my spiritual twin, Kendra.

"What you want, hooker?" Kendra spat over the line.

"Just checking on you, slut," I threw back.

We both paused for a moment, then burst out laughing.

"Really, what's up with you, girl?" Kendra asked. "You did say three, right?"

"Well, um…"

"Oh, I just know you're not calling to cancel on me when today is my only day off! I just know you aren't gonna diss me like that."

"Kendraaaaa…you know I wouldn't cancel unless it was something I couldn't control, and—"

"You cheat!"

I laughed. "How am I a cheat?"

Kendra smacked her lips sarcastically. "You told me you were fixing beef stew. You know I love your beef stew. Shoot, I was already tasting those potatoes!"

"I'm sorry, boo-boo," I said in a feigned baby voice. "I'll make it up to you, I promise. When are you off again? Damnit!" I pushed hard on my brakes when a Ford Escort stopped without warning in front of me.

"What's wrong?"

"Nothing." I sighed. "This traffic is just crazy."

"Oh, okay. Well, drive carefully, child. Don't want nothing to happen to you. But I'm not off again till next week. I have a conference in College Park tomorrow through Friday. So…I guess you're out of luck. But what are you doing going to work? I thought you were off most Sundays?"

My mind was everywhere: traffic, Kendra, Kyte, beef stew. I felt so relieved when I finally was about to pull into the parking lot at the FBI headquarters. Other than a few scattered vehicles it was almost empty.

"Like I was told, when it comes to FBI work, there are

no days off. But look, I'm at headquarters. I'll call you when I leave. Maybe we can meet up and have dessert and coffee at Ruby's or something."

"Make it Outback's and you've got a deal. I'm suddenly craving some deep, dark chocolate cake from the land Down Under."

I laughed. "Okay, Dr. Gray, I'll talk to you later."

I pushed the off button on my cell phone. Never would I tire of conversation with my sharp-tongued college friend. But now it was time to see what was so important to Kyte that he would risk pissing me off by taking away my Sunday. I figured it had to be something big.

When I got to his office I was surprised to see he was alone, other than his assistant, Missy. Kyte always felt that if he had to work, everybody had to work.

I tapped softly on the opened door.

"Yoo-hoo! What are you doing in there?" I peeked inside, caught Kyte's eye, and smiled.

"About time you got here," he said.

He pulled me into a big bear hug. I hugged him back. Even though I hesitated to admit it, I loved Kyte. He was one of my favorite people. He was certainly the most respected agent we had in the East Coast division. The respect he earned was not only because of his prowess as an agent, but also for the fact that he actually cared about everyone who worked under him, on a personal level.

"You smell like beef," Kyte said, sniffing.

I scowled at his feeble attempt at teasing and looked at him with a suspicious eye. "So why am I here?" I asked.

"Can't I just miss you?"

"Can't you just tell me what's up?"

"Okay, okay," Kyte said. His face lost its smile as he reached for an envelope and waved it at me. He knew that with me, it was best to get straight to the point.

"Hmm…" I took the envelope from him and quickly peeped at its contents.

There were three black-and-white photos inside, all of one black man—a dead black man. I quickly read the statement about his death. There were no definite conclusions, but it had been ruled a homicide.

"Okay, and who is this poor soul?" I asked, looking up at Kyte.

"He was found in a hotel room in Bowie, Maryland, two days ago. His name is Kaseem Soroco."

"So how was he killed?"

"That's just it. There aren't any visible marks or any reason that a healthy twenty-five-year-old male should just die of heart failure. There was nothing that showed a struggle, no stab wounds, no gunshot wounds, nothing."

"Okay, so my next question is, why are we involved in a local murder case? Shouldn't this be handled by the state?"

Kyte handed me another file. *Top Secret* was printed on the folder cover with the code *Nigeria*. The problems the U.S.A. had with Nigeria were front-page news. Tension was high due to tribal strife. The U.S. President's insistence in gaining control over the threatened coup made relations with most African governments chilly, especially Nigeria.

"Looks like this could be a huge problem." I pursed my lips in concentration. "Is there any proof that it was politically motivated?"

"Kim, we don't have anything at all. Why do you think I got you out of the house so quickly? The president wants this investigated. He wants it done immediately."

The door to Kyte's office opened. A smiling Micah Latimer walked in.

"And you and Latimer are the just the remedy we need to take care of this impending germ," Kyte continued.

"Hey, Micah," I said in greeting.

He winked back at me, then took the case files out of my hand and started reading over the same odd, yet intriguing synopsis of the case. Micah had the most interesting face. Thin lines creased his forehead as he concentrated. It almost made me laugh, watching him. His dark brown skin shone in clear unblemished color. Micah was attractive for sure. But it was his personality that was the most attractive. Not to mention the tiny dimples that brightened his smile. He looked up at Kyte and me with a frown.

"What if this is not what we're thinking? What if it's a local murder?" he asked.

"I told Kyte the same thing."

"Well…" Kyte moved over to his desk and sat in his huge leather chair. "That's what I want you two to find

out. You know I'm thinking that with your Nigerian back-
ground, you could easily pass for a native."

"Why would I want to pass for a native?" Micah
asked, laughing.

"There's a party scheduled for—" he paused and looked
down at his pad "—this coming Friday. I want you two
there. Kimberla can go as your date. There will be mostly
diplomats there and political allies."

"So this is a Nigerian party? What do you want us to
find out?" I queried.

"Whatever you can do, do it. Ask questions, you two
know the ropes. But until then I want you to investigate
behind the scenes, too. Find out as much as you can about
Soroco. Whatever you do, I want this shit off us. The president wants any suspicion cleared."

I looked at Micah. It would be fun working with him
again. The question was, would he have fun working with
me, knowing how bossy I could be?

"You think you can manage dealing with me for a few
weeks, partner?" I asked him hesitantly.

"Sure. I always did love a challenge." He winked.

CHAPTER 2

Jacob

Time had not been my friend for the last month and a half. I wanted to get home. In fact, I never wanted to leave in the first place. For some reason I had lost my enthusiasm for the job. It had felt like that ever since the Michael Riley case. And no matter how I tried to shake the shitty feelings that crept over me, I just couldn't.

I drove to Kimberla's house feeling a nervous excitement coursing through me. I couldn't wait to see her, and more than that, I couldn't wait to hold her again.

I jumped out of my Lexus and reached into the backseat for the dozen red roses I had stopped and purchased for her. Normally I wasn't an overly romantic brotha. And even when I did try to get mushy, Kimberla would squash that notion. But tonight was special; tonight was a surprise. I was, in fact, a week ahead of time with my homecoming and wanted to get an amorous reaction from her. The flowers were just my way of showing her how much I missed her and how much she meant to me.

Slowly I pulled up to her apartment complex. With it

being Sunday and after 7:00 p.m., I was surprised to see that her car wasn't in her drive. Meaning she wasn't home. Disappointment surfaced in me, but I squashed it quickly and pulled into an empty guest spot where I figured she wouldn't think to look. I grabbed the flowers from my backseat and decided I would let myself in and wait for her.

Her apartment looked like her, smelled like her, and the distinctive purr of my cat, Blu, gave me even more familiarity.

"Hey, girl," I said with a smile. I grabbed her up, rubbing her blue-gray coat of fur as she cuddled against my neck. It felt so good to be home and away from the chaos of Chicago. I allowed Blu to jump out of my arms, and walked into the kitchen, searching for a vase to put Kimberla's flowers in. As soon as I found one in the kitchen cabinet, I heard the front door unlock. I walked back toward the living room, stopping at the entryway and leaning against it.

"And where have you been?" I said to her in a soft voice.

Kimberla jumped. "Jacob!"

"Hey, baby." My slow smile started inside and spread all over my face. She was still as lovely as ever. Kimberla wasn't necessarily a pretty woman. But she was beautiful in a strong, yet feminine way. She stood there watching me, speechless. So I walked over to her and picked her up in one scoop. Her long legs wrapped around me in an instant.

"Surprised?"

"Oh my God!" she crooned as she buried her face in my neck. She grabbed my face between both hands and kissed my lips for a long, sensual moment.

I walked backward, still holding her, and fell back on the couch. "Mmm, babe. Did you miss me?" I asked again as she wiggled against me. My body naturally hardened.

"What do you think? I didn't expect you for two more weeks!"

"There was an early break in the case. I thought I would surprise you." I smiled. "I've known what day I was coming back since last week."

"Well, you kept a beautiful secret." Kimberla's voice almost broke. She seemed happy to see me, but there was a hesitancy about her that was slightly confusing. It was almost as if she didn't want to look directly at me.

I grabbed her chin, forcing her eyes to meet mine. I took one of her hands and gave it a Lancelot kiss. "Well, you knew I was counting the days to get back to you."

She blushed and looked away. "Well, um…I didn't get a chance to finish dinner. I wish I had. You have to be hungry." She bit her lip.

Kimberla looked uncomfortable. Why? I couldn't quite put my finger on it. She tried to pull away so she could get up, but I held her fast to me.

"What?" She laughed again.

"You still haven't told me that you missed me."

"Yes, I did."

"You did not. You asked, what do I think? That is not an answer. Did you miss me?"

"Yes, Jacob White, I missed you…. Now tell me what happened with your case."

"Well, there's not a lot to tell. My part was mostly behind the scenes. You know I had no problem with that. I didn't want to go in the first place."

"It's just good to have you home again," she said. She buried her face against my neck.

"Stand up," I whispered, pushing her away slightly. I knew exactly what I wanted—needed to do to her.

"What?" she whispered back, standing up.

I kissed her belly and then got up myself. I grabbed her hand and led her to the back of the love seat couch we had been sitting on. After looking in her eyes for a moment, I got down on my knees in front of her.

"What are you doing?"

Kimberla's breathing increased in speed when I lifted her miniskirt. If she hadn't been aware before of what I was doing, by now she had to be. I had been burning for this woman's touch the whole time I was away, dreaming about it, feenin' like a crack addict for the sweetness between her legs. She had on thin bikini panties. I licked her through the fabric. The dampness of the material told me she was already wet and wanting me. She moaned when my lips touched her, and I licked again, sucking her love through the material till I could feel her clitoris swelling. I sucked it into my mouth.

"Ohhh, Jacob!" she gasped. Her hips jerked against my lips. "Oh, Jacob, oh yes!"

She bucked and grabbed my head for leverage. This was what I wanted. This fuel, this— I used my mouth to push the material of her panties aside so I could feel and taste her without boundaries. I could feel her shaking, so I gripped her hips and lifted her onto the top of the sofa back and started slurping at her opening. My dick was throbbing, tingling. Damn, she turned me on. I dug my tongue inside her. In and out, in and out, causing her to scream out.

"Mmm...baby," she moaned. "Please don't stop." I flicked my tongue against her swollen bud and sucked it into my mouth, licking and slurping from her opening to her clit, demanding her release. I could tell by the way her hips were thrusting against me that she was about to come.

"Yeah, baby," I purred against her. "Come for me."

She moaned at my words. Her back fell against the sofa and her hips moved up and down against my mouth as she spasmed again and again and again. I held her there till she stopped trembling, and then pulled her down on the floor and into my arms, kissing the sweat from her forehead.

"I guess you did miss something about me." I laughed softly.

"Whatever!" She punched me on the arm good-naturedly. "Stop it, you know better than that." She looked at me and winked. "Come into my chamber and I'll show you something else..."

"Oh yeah?" I teased. "Whatcha gonna show me?"

She got up and began walking toward her bedroom. She didn't even have to wonder if I was coming behind her. Kimberla knew she had me on lock.

* * *

Catwomyn75

She knew what time her new cyberlover was going to be signing on. That was one thing about the men who visited the chat room. They were on a constant clock. Most of them would come online while at work. Some were married, and hiding their cheating ways from the wife. Some had girlfriends, and some were just too fickle to stick with one woman. Some of them just simply couldn't stay away from the gay chat rooms. That's where she came in; that's where she found David a.k.a. Urban_Dreams.

She signed on invisible, but could see who was on her e-mail friends' list. She clicked over to the alias name she used when she frequented Gay Chats. Of course David was there. He would be in the black DL undercover room for bisexual men. He was always in there, creeping. *DLSucka82* was the name she used. She never communicated under that name. But she watched and she listened, and she learned, and she found David. She switched over to the name he truly knew her by and she IMed him.

Catwomyn75: Hello, David.

Urban_Dreams: What's going on, ma?

Catwomyn75: You tell me.

Urban_Dreams: What are you talking about? lol.

Catwomyn75: I get the feeling you didn't like what you saw on cam the other night.

Urban_Dreams: Oh come on, you know you look good.

Catwomyn75: So...meet me.

Urban_Dreams: When? Tonight?

Catwomyn75: I don't want to meet for tea. If we're gonna do this, I want more than a hello and a smile. Feel me?

Urban_Dreams: Shit. I want more than that, too. Trust me. So where do you want to meet?

She paused. Tonight was perfect. The fact that he was open to things made her smile and laugh at the same time.

Catwomyn75: Can you meet me in fifteen minutes?

Urban_Dreams: Sho can.

Catwomyn75: Wonderful. Get some paper and write down this address.

Urban_Dreams: Aight, ma. Hold on a minute.

Men. They were such stupid, gullible creatures.

David wasn't used to meeting strange women off the Internet. There was just something about this one that plucked his interest. She wouldn't send a picture, but she had gotten on a Web cam briefly. What he saw assured him that he was meeting a beautiful, sexy woman, and not some faking beach whale.

He pulled up at the hotel address she had given him. This should be an interesting sexual experience, he thought. A dark-blue Jeep Liberty pulled up beside his truck. The beautiful long-legged creature that got out of it had his heart beating in a rush almost immediately.

"Did you get a room already?" she asked him, leaning into his window.

"I was waiting for you."

"Well, go on, do your thing. I'll wait for you out here." She smiled provocatively. She moved back from his truck so that he could get out.

"I'll be right back," he told her.

He rushed inside. He felt lucky that they had an available room without a reservation. But David kind of figured she wouldn't want that anyhow. She seemed to him to be the married kind. That was all right. He had tumbled with married women before. It didn't bother him to be some lucky female's side thing, or Spackavelli, like the song goes. He laughed to himself thinking about the lyrics to the song. *A brotha who would love her when her man ain't doing her right.* Yeah, he'd be that.

David was excited as he made his way back to his internet lover. She was waiting for him in her car. Her leg was hanging out the door, her shapely calf flexed at him. He motioned for her to follow him.

"This is nice," she said when they got into the room.

It was rather plush for a budget hotel. A Chinese patterned bedspread covered the bed. There were matching lamp shades haloing the antique lamps that sat upon the tables.

Desire coated David's eyes as his date walked into the hotel room. She called herself Jami. The name fit, as far as he was concerned. But he somehow got the feeling it was not her real name. He looked down at her left hand. No ring. There was a tan line, showing where there had been one, though. David laughed.

"What?" she asked.

"Nothing." David motioned to her with his finger. "Come here."

Jami swiveled over to him, keeping her eyes planted on his. When she was standing in front of him, she immediately began unzipping his pants.

"What a minute!" David moaned. He moaned louder when Jami grabbed his dick, rubbing it up and down in her hand. Before he knew it, she pushed him back onto the bed.

"Turn over," she said. "Turn on your stomach."

"No. I wanna watch you."

"Wouldn't you rather feel me than watch me? Turn over. I have a surprise for you. Trust me, you're gonna love it."

David's heart started to race. He swallowed a moan as her lips grabbed his. There was something about this woman, something wild and exciting. But even more so, there was something evil about her. That evil spirit turned him on.

She pushed her body closer to his. From the corner of

his eye David saw something shining. He turned around and was about to see what it was, but instead something told him to look at Jami's eyes. The hypnotic look he felt before no longer turned him on. He felt a chill run through him and he pushed her off. Then he felt a stinging pinprick pain in his neck.

"What the fuck are you doing?" he screamed.

Jami fell to the bed beside him, smiling, still looking at him with that iniquitous expression. And David, he felt paralyzed, frozen—immobilized. His body would not move. Then he no longer felt fear.

He felt nothing.

CHAPTER 3

Jacob

I was breathless as I fell back against the silk covers on Kimberla's bed. My heart was still racing. I had to gulp a couple of times to get my mental balance. And even though I had come, the feeling of her heat surrounding me was still like heaven.

"Are you okay?" Kimberla whispered.

"No—no. I guess I'm not," I stammered back. Hell, I couldn't even hide what I felt for her. After all these months, being with her, getting to know her person and definitely her strength. She took me places emotionally that I hadn't been in so long. She made me feel weak.

But there was one problem. What does a man do when all his "I love you's" never earn him an "I love you, too"? I knew she had feelings for me, without a doubt. But she never said it. It was never voiced. Sometimes she would joke and say, "Ditto. Awww, aren't you sweet?" Or something that let me know it wasn't serious to her. But my feelings were real. This had been an ongoing problem, yet one of the reasons I took the job in Chicago was that I was hoping that the "absence makes the heart grow fonder" adage would apply in Kimberla's case. For some reason it seemed that even after our making love, something was still missing, and I couldn't put my finger on it. It was almost as if she was okay with the companionship and the sex, but she wouldn't let me past her wall, or whatever it was she had protecting her heart. Her coolness, the push-and-pull way she handled her emotions were starting to eat at me. You can give your all for only so long, receiving nothing in return, before you start putting up walls of your own.

"You seem so preoccupied."

I looked at her and smiled, trying to erase the disturbing thoughts that had been flowing through my mind. I looked down at her lips. "Do I? Well, I dunno." I sighed a little. "Maybe I just hoped you were a little happier to have me back."

"What?" Kimberla sat up. A puzzled look came over her face. "Jacob, I'm very happy that you're back. Why would you even say that?"

"I don't know. It just feels like you're so *whatever* about it. Do you realize we have spent the last hour and a half together and I have said I love you so many times, but you have not once said it back?" I cleared my throat, then moved to get up. "Maybe I should be used to it by now. I dunno…"

Kimberla stretched languidly and eyed me with amusement. I suddenly felt sorry that I had said anything. Thinking about it is one thing. Giving up your balls and letting a woman know she is making you feel like shit is another.

"Baby, why you getting into your feelings?" she mused. "We just finished making love. And now you're saying I'm not happy to have you back? That's silly!"

"You know, I knew you would do this."

"Do what?"

I grabbed the robe that I kept at her house and tied it around my waist. "I knew you would make a joke of it. Play me off when I'm being real with you. I'm serious..."

I sat back on the bed beside her.

"And so am I. You know, for a man, you can be so sentimental at times." Kimberla slid over, scissoring me with her long legs. "Listen, I couldn't be happier to have you back. And I missed you desperately." She grabbed my chin, bringing her lips close to mine. "Okay?"

Before I could respond, the phone rang. Oh, hell naw, I thought. We had to talk. As much as I regretted opening up this discussion, now that it was open, I wanted to finish it.

"Don't answer it," I whispered.

Kimberla kissed my lips. "I have to, baby. I have a new case I'm working on and it could be Kyte or Micah Latimer."

"Micah Latimer? Huh?" I reached out, grabbing her hand, trying to hold her from getting up. "Just let it ring, please?"

It was too late, she was already saying hello. I sighed,

got up, and walked into the bathroom. I could hear her conversation as I washed my face.

"Micah? What's going on?"

I walked back into the bedroom. Kimberla looked up at me, giving me a worried look. Obviously she was not worried enough, I thought, since she was still yapping away with Latimer. *Why the hell was my face getting hot?*

"Oh no! Is it another Nigerian?" she asked him. "Okay, give me thirty minutes. I'm on my way now." She hung up.

"On your way where?" I asked, not able to keep the bite out of my tone.

"Baby, I got to go. They found a body at a hotel over by Security Boulevard. It could have something to do with the Soroco case."

"You haven't even told me anything about what you're working on, and I just got back, Kimberla. This is ridiculous!"

"Come on, Jacob." She placed her hand on my cheek. "Try to understand, okay? You know how this goes. I'll be back as soon as I can."

My jaw clenched as Kimberla made her way to the bathroom.

"Yeah," I whispered to myself. "I know how it goes."

Kimberla

The flashing lights of police vehicles brightened the already heavily lit street. A crowd had started to gather as I pulled up into the hotel parking lot. A group of the boys in blue and also uniformed agents blocked the civilian crowd.

I got out of my car and flashed my badge at the Baltimore policeman that tried to block me. I smirked a little when he let me past. The power of an FBI badge was intoxicating, even though most locals hated us getting involved. I quickly made my way inside the hotel and to the crime scene.

"Damn, can't we do anything ourselves without you people sticking your nose in shit?"

I turned around to the voice of Larry McNeal, who was the chief of police in Baltimore.

"Well, if it isn't my favorite little boy in blue," I said with a saccharine smile. He gave me an icy stare and then stepped aside.

Inside the room was a black male, slim build, dark-skinned complexion. His eyes were open. It was obviously a quick death. His pants were loosened and his shirt was up over his abdomen.

Micah Latimer walked up beside me as I was examining the victim.

"Still don't know the exact cause of death," he stated. "But look here." He pointed to the victim's neck. There was a red mark, bloodied and swollen.

"What do you think that is?" I asked.

"I don't know," Micah said, seeming as perplexed as I was. "But it doesn't look like there was much of a struggle."

I looked over at the side table by the bed. There sat a

condom, his wallet, a pack of Newport 100s, and his car keys. Glancing at the victim again, I also noticed that his belt was unbuckled and his zipper was down.

"Hmm...the killer is a woman," I stated flatly.

"Bingo. Or either a woman is involved somehow," Micah Latimer agreed.

"So you think more than one person was involved here? And what the hell is this on his neck?" I examined the mark, which looked like a slightly risen welt.

Micah's eyebrows rose in concentration. "Sting gun? Who knows?"

We backed away from the body once the crime-scene photographers came in to snap their photos, and we took notes on how he was killed. A man wouldn't have done it so delicately. This was a planned murder. A woman did it, who was in no way stupid or a heat-of-the-moment type of person. He was led here, and the killer knew exactly what she was going to do.

"Have you talked with the front desk clerk?" I asked.

"Sure did. She says that he checked in by himself. There was nobody with him. Maybe the murderer waited in the car."

"Probably so," I noted.

"Hmm..." Micah continued staring at the victim. "Well, let's check in with crime scene later to find out what evidence they gathered. We can get out of here. Are we still on for Wednesday night?"

"Of course we are—especially now."

"You think this murder may have to do with the Soroco case?" Micah said thoughtfully.

"You think maybe you are jumping to conclusions? We don't automatically want to start screaming serial murder, right?"

"I don't know, but anyhow, let's see what we can come up with and move on from there."

Jacob

After Kimberla left me in her bed alone all kinds of thoughts played on my mind; negative ones. I decided it would be better for me to rest in my own bed rather than laying there trippin' and feeling like somebody's last thought. It bothered me that I felt so unsure of my steps when it came to that woman. Because it wasn't me; not Jacob White. Not even with my late wife had I gone to such odd degrees of private desperation that I found myself doing with Kimberla. But then again, with her, I never had to wonder if the love was returned, either...

The door crackled as I let myself into my apartment. In the darkness of the night I set Blu's cage down at the door, ignoring her purrs for release. She gave another cat moan.

"Sorry, girl," I lamented.

Blu was too old and set in her ways to get her feathers ruffled. Kind of like Kimberla, I thought with a chuckle. Although she wasn't old, she was definitely set in her ways. I really was surprised that she and Blu hadn't gotten along better with them being so much alike.

I sighed, flicking on the light and tossing my keys on the coffee table. I moved Blu's cage down beside my dark blue sectional and let her out of the entrapment. She walked out slowly, stretching her furry back into a hump.

"Yeah," I said aloud to myself. "Just like Kimmy."

My thoughts instantly went to the way she stretched and purred when I loved her just right, letting me know I was hitting her spot.

I went into my bedroom and flopped on the king-size sleigh bed. It had been almost two months since I'd spent a night sleeping in my own bed. My last assignment had been a short but tedious one. My mission was basically backing another agent who had gotten himself into trouble. It was nothing like my previous assignment. I grew somber just thinking about that. The success I had gained in nabbing and shutting down Michael Riley's criminal empire earned me respect with the bureau. But for some reason it still wasn't enough, not for me at least. I had put my all into that case and worked hard to get Riley.

Oddly enough, Michael, in his own way, had love for me, that philia type of love for a brother. I guess he loved as much as any criminal was capable of doing. As much as I hated Michael's actions, I had fondness for him, too. I couldn't keep my mind off that case. When he died, it was hard for me to deal with; it was hard having had close company with someone for over a year, have him call you brother, and not be affected by his demise. More than once, since then, I had thought about why I was still an agent. My original plans had been to quit after New York, but of course it hadn't turned out like that. A successful sting can make you in demand, and that had sort of happened to me. I guess I should have been flattered. But at this point, a brotha was just tired.

I fell across my bed in a tired heap. It didn't take me long to start dozing off, but just as I was sleeping, the phone rang. I jumped up, rubbing my eyes at the sleep disruption.

"Hello?" I said groggily, holding the receiver half to my ear.

"Jacob White. Well, well, well."

"Lawd. I know this voice!"

"You'd better know it…"

"How are you, Lolita?" I felt myself smiling.

"I'm better now that I'm talking to you," she flirted. "I've missed you, baby. L.A. was never the same after you left."

Lolita Mason put the *S* in special agent. I had worked with her for a couple of years in Los Angeles. It was a fact that Lolita's ability to work under pressure was only matched by, well, Kimberla Bacon's. And I had the utmost respect for her. Not to mention she was gorgeous. She and I had dated off and on, briefly, if one wished to call it that. It wasn't really serious, just the typical wining and dining and getting yo freak on.

"So what are you up to now?" I asked. I fiddled with the pattern of the bedspread with my toe, and then looked over at the clock. I again started to wonder if, or when, Kimberla would call me.

"Did you hear what I just said?"

"Oh, I'm sorry." I sat up abruptly. "What was that again?"

"Damn, I feel so loved," Lolita said with a laugh. "I said...I'm in D.C."

"What are you doing in D.C.?"

"I live here now. I told you, honey, I was ready for a change. When I saw the chance to come East, I took it. Are you surprised?"

I could sense her sarcastic smile. "Nothing about you surprises me, Lolita. Are you here visiting or here to stay?"

"Invite me over for some late-night Black and Decker and I'll tell you."

"Black and Decker?"

"Coffee, you fool." She laughed.

"Well, actually I have a Mr. Coffee."

"Just give me the address and we can debate coffeemakers later."

I thought about it, looked over at the clock, and laughed. Maybe a chill moment with an old friend was just what the doctor ordered. And maybe, just maybe, it would also help get my mind off Kimberla.

CHAPTER 4

Kimberla

I was tired and pissed, and if I may say so, felt a bit guilty when I got to my apartment. Jacob had left, which surprised me, but at the same time I kind of understood it. I knew I had some making up to do. I had run out on him in such a rush, and of course that pissed him off; hurt him maybe? I left as soon as I realized he wasn't there, and headed to his place. I had to make him understand that his feelings were unnecessary. The man had to know I was happy to have him home, but as a fellow agent, why couldn't he be more understanding about my position? Our jobs as agents always took precedence over personal issues—always!

I pulled up to the front of his condo. I immediately felt something was wrong. There was a car in his visitor's parking spot, a spot that was normally reserved for me. I was also surprised because it was close to midnight.

"Who the hell could you have visiting you this time of the morning, man?" I said out loud to myself.

When I got out of my car, a breeze washed over my face. I went up to his door and rung the bell over and over again. Almost feeling desperate. Somehow the weather, which had been clear just moments before, seemed cloudy now. It could have been my temperature that was changing. I felt hot inside. I knew he had someone in there with him, and some unknown feeling inside told me that it was not someone of his own sex. My throat felt dry as I waited. Things were too damn quiet. Was he having sex with someone? I got dizzy at the thought. I just knew Jacob was not the type of man who would make love to me and be running up in some other woman hours later; he couldn't be! I wasn't that poor a judge of character, but then again, if that was the truth, why did I make such poor choices in the past, and why was I feeling like my world was about to crumble into tiny little pieces?

I rang the bell again. After what felt like five minutes he opened the door.

"Hey," he said, looking surprised. "What are you doing here? It got so late I didn't even expect you to call."

I ignored him and pushed my way into his apartment. "Do you know someone is parked in your guest spot?"

"Yeah, I do, I—"

He didn't have to say another word. There on his living room couch sat a high-yellow creature sipping a cup of coffee out of the mug that I had given him as a house-warming gift for his new condo. The freakin' nerve!

I didn't get a chance to ask who the chick was. Jacob was right on it.

"Kimberla, this is Lolita. She and I used to work in the

West Coast division in L.A. Remember I'd mentioned her to you once?" he asked nervously.

His voice sounded very hollow to me, and very nervous. The Lolita creature stood up, then walked over to me, hand extended for a shake.

"Hello, Agent Bacon. Jacob, really there's no need for an introduction. Everyone has heard of the famed Chameleon." She smiled.

I didn't smile back, nor did I shake her hand. Impatiently I waited for an explanation of this late-night excursion. It was hard to concentrate on the full situation. I was too busy making careful note of the woman and wondering if this was the type of female that Jacob normally dated. Petite, redboned, J-Lo booty, slanted hazel-green eyes. The woman's obvious beauty made me feel like one of Cinderella's stepsisters. It made me feel like the tall, dark, ugly duckling that I had always seen myself as.

Seeming to feel the chill in the air, Lolita said, "Well, I guess I'll be going…" She cautiously looked over at Jacob.

Even that pissed me off. I was boiling inside. And I, Kimberla Bacon, never, ever lost my cool, especially not over some woman!

Who are you kidding, Kimberla? There never has been another man you felt like this about that you would get jealous over.

"You don't have to rush off, Lolita," Jacob said.

"Oh, I think she does," I said flatly.

I was a rock, unmoving as Jacob walked Lolita to the

door. I didn't even look in their direction, but my head swung around in a whip fashion once I heard the door close.

"How dare you!" I spat, my voice gurgling from hurt. "How dare you play me like this? What was that woman doing here this time of the night? Huh, Jacob? Huh?"

Jacob walked up to me, sighing slightly. "Calm down, Kimmy. She is a friend, someone I used to work with. She's relocated here and she just came by to say hi and have a cup of coffee, that's all."

"Nobody comes over at midnight unless it's for a booty call, unless she's looking for some dick!"

"Don't talk like that."

"Don't talk like what?" I almost screamed.

"Vulgar, nasty. It doesn't even sound like you. And regardless of how you may look at it, I'm telling you the truth. It was just a cup of coffee!"

"Do you think I'm stupid? How long was I gone before you hooked up with another woman, huh?"

"She is a friend," Jacob said solemnly.

"Yeah, she's a friend, and I'm the freaking pope!"

Jacob walked up to me with an attempt to wrap his arms around me. His hands made me feel as if I had been burnt. I caught my breath as I held back the tears, disgusted at his touch.

"Don't," I croaked, pushing him back.

His hands dropped heavily to his sides. "So you just want to believe that I would cheat on you? Does it make you feel better thinking that when you know it's not true?"

"I don't know anything. All I know is no woman with any common sense would be okay with her man having another woman at his house at midnight. And why you would think I would be okay with that is beyond me."

I walked up to the front door and gripped my keys tightly. "Listen, I'm going to go. It's been a long day and I'm tired."

"Okay, but please believe me, Kimmy. I wouldn't do that to you. I swear it."

I looked up at the pleading look on his face. Did it even matter? We weren't married. He didn't owe me anything. I didn't owe him anything. I didn't have the time or energy for the drama, either way. My anger suddenly evaporated, and all I felt was limp exhaustion.

I couldn't even meet his eyes as I finally said, "I'll call you tomorrow."

"Kim—"

"Really, it's fine," I said, cutting him off. "I'll call you tomorrow."

I gave him one last smothering look of hurt, and left, shutting the door soundly behind me. Once I was in my car I didn't know if I wanted to cry or throw up. I sat there gripping the steering wheel so tightly my knuckles turned white. One thing for sure I did know, I was not going to allow myself to go through pain and doubt over any man. I couldn't, I wouldn't. Not even for Jacob.

It's difficult to ignore the smell of death. There is an un-mistakable finality about it. A pungent odor that is just as mental as it is physical. And no amount of deodorizer can disguise its power.

The sound of our steps was a hollow echo as Micah and I walked down the hallway leading to the examination room. We had been called to discuss the findings by medical examiner Shane Weedon. She had performed the autopsy on David Rivers, our latest murder victim.

Both Micah and I felt the politicians who were suspicious that the Soroco case was politically motivated were wrong. David Rivers's murder was not a welcome one, but it did finally add some weight to the suspicion that this could be a domestic problem. I personally couldn't decide what was worse. Either way, we needed some answers.

We walked into the room. Shane stood over Rivers's body. His coloring was blanched, his lips blue. There was what one calls a dog tag hanging from his right big toe. The examiner had his chest wide open. My stomach curled and I swallowed back nausea. No matter how many years I spent as an agent, I would never get used to that smell.

"So what have you found?" Micah queried.

Shane looked up and pushed her bifocals up on her nose. "Heart attack."

"Heart attack?" I repeated.

"Yes. Here is a thirty-year-old, healthy man who appears to have worked out religiously. According to his medical records he had no previous heart condition. Hadn't been sick a day in his life."

Micah laughed. "Maybe he was about to get down

with who he thought was a woman and got a surprise. Shocked him into an attack. I know it would me."

"Micah, please." I gave him a scolding look.

"Well, you never know." He laughed again.

Shane cut in. "I will tell you two this, the scratch on his neck? It's a needle mark. So chances are he was poisoned. The question is, with what?"

"And you haven't been able to find out?" I asked.

"No," Shane said, shaking her head. "There are no traces of anything abnormal in his bloodstream. That's what's so puzzling about this."

Micah leaned closer to Rivers's body, again examining the scratch on his neck. He slipped a lollipop in his mouth and began to suck on it slowly. How he could even think about eating anything at this moment was beyond my imagination. I swallowed back an automatic hurl reflex.

Ignoring Micah, I addressed Shane again. "So do you think, as we kind of do, that it's the same MO as the Soroco case?"

"That I don't know. You see, the family wouldn't allow us to do an autopsy."

"What!" Micah exclaimed.

Shane nodded. "His body was sent back to Nigeria. The family insisted on it."

Micah and I looked at each other at the same time, in disbelief.

"So why do you think Kyte didn't tell us about this?" he said, mirroring my thoughts.

"I don't know," I seethed. I was totally pissed that Kyte would insist we get to the bottom of the case, and yet hold back vital information that could help us do just that!

"So how long do you think it will take you to find out what killed this guy?" Micah asked Shane.

"Who? Soroco?"

"No!" Micah spat in frustration. I almost chuckled at his expression as he pointed to Rivers's body. "Dead dude right there."

I glanced over at Shane to hear what her response would be. She looked back down at the victim's body and started rubbing her fingers across the needle mark on his neck.

"Well," she said, "there are many different substances that could have been used. I need to do some more lab work and tests. But I would definitely say he was murdered." She looked up at us, opening her hands in a question. "We'll just have to see, right? But I'll get back to you two by tomorrow."

Ten minutes later, I sat in my car struggling to shield my eyes from the evening sunrays. I felt so confused about both murder cases, and I could tell that Micah did, too. He had been talking nonstop ever since we had left Shane Weedon. Mostly he was upset, as I also was, that Kyte had not informed us that Soroco's body had been flown out.

I tried not to sigh out loud, and listened to him rant for ten full minutes. I had other personal matters on my mind, namely Jacob.

The past couple of days had been difficult for us. I guess I had gotten over his indiscretion. I tried to convince myself of that. But I really tried not to put too much thought into it. With all the time I was spending with Micah on the murder cases, I didn't have time for personal headaches. Being busy helped a lot. I had only seen Jacob once since Sunday night, and the topic of Lolita had not been brought up again. I smiled a little inside. Jacob knew me well enough to know that when I didn't want to talk about something, that meant the subject was closed, period. Wisely, he'd left it alone. Things had been stiff and chilly between us, but he had said he understood my being busy. Actually at this point, at this time, that's all he could say. What else could he do other than deal with my wrath? Jacob knew I could be a queen bee if pushed.

I realized that I was visibly wandering again when Micah asked, "What's wrong? Am I boring you or something?"

"No, it's not you. I was just thinking about Jacob."

"Hmm…" He looked at me from the corner of his eye. "You women kill me."

"What?"

"You tell a man you forgive him, yet you keep him in the doghouse."

"He's not in the doghouse," I said, rolling my eyes.

"But he hasn't been in your bed, either, has he?"

I didn't respond. I was tired and I rubbed my eyes, hoping he would let the subject go.

"Look, babe, I thought you said you believed him about the chick."

"I *do* believe him."

"So what's the problem?"

My cell phone vibrated and then kicked out the sounds of Fantasia's "Baby Mama."

Micah laughed when he heard it. "Leave it to you to have that song as a ring tone."

Ignoring him, I teasingly poked out my tongue, then answered my cell with a soft "Hello?"

It was Jacob. I made a face and shushed Micah when he whispered, "Uh-oh."

"Kimmy, where are you? You were supposed to meet me for dinner an hour ago."

"Ugh, I completely forgot!" I looked at my watch and bit my lip. Damnit! It was already 7:30 p.m. "Can we just meet for lunch tomorrow? I'm really tired and it's been a busy day."

Jacob was quiet for a long time. I felt my throat tightening. I absolutely hated the tension between us.

"Are you still there?" I whispered.

"Yeah, I am. So is there a reason that I can't come over, then? We could cuddle a little. You always love that. Maybe look at some TV?"

I pulled up at the light and closed my eyes. A strong spring wind blazed through the car window, alleviating some of my stress, but not much. Jacob was a man, and like all men, he wouldn't be kept at bay forever. I didn't even know exactly what was wrong with me. Was it really all about Lolita? Did I really not trust him, or really feel he was cheating on me? All kinds of thoughts rambled through my mind. And I was silent.

"Look," he finally said, "I'll just call you tomorrow." He sounded hurt, and it saddened me to hear his pain and confusion, but still... "Good night, Kimmy." He hung up the phone.

I closed the flip lid to my phone and stuffed it inside my purse. I could feel Micah eyeballing me.

"Don't say a word," I said.

He was examining his manicured nails. He was probably trying to think of something sarcastic or witty to say. Anything to let me know I was wrong.

"I wasn't going to say anything. I mean, I won't say a word about how you are messing up with a good brotha. I won't say a word about you stirring up trouble in your paradise. Burning down your valley of heaven, kicking the brotha in the balls and unmanning him. I'm just gonna sit here and mind my own business."

"So why are you still talking?" I almost screamed. He opened his mouth to say something else. "Shut up, Micah."

At that, he closed it.

CHAPTER 5

Kimberla

She was running. Falling with every two steps, trying to get away from him. Although she couldn't see him, she could hear him; she could smell him. He was calling her, haunting her with his whispery voice. Her breath was coming in heavy heaves. She made her way down the hallway, to the bedroom, and had almost gotten the door slammed shut before it came crashing back open. The force knocked her to the floor. Her head banged hard against the wooden sideboard of the bed. She looked up. He was coming down on her, his eyes piercing.

"Why'd you run, girl?"

"Please," she cried. "Don't—don't."

Ignored, she could feel his weight heavy on top of her, his privates grinding roughly against her own. The hands that she once dreamed of holding tenderly now ripped at her panties, tearing them from her body. She cried when he jammed his fingers inside her. She couldn't believe that this was the same boy who only an hour ago had made her heart beat fast just at the thought of him. She couldn't

believe he had changed that fast from being her fantasy to
her nightmare. He yanked her face toward his, and as his
mouth came down over hers, her screams were muffled.

I woke up sweating, but that sweat was also mixed with tears that chased down my cheeks. I caught my breath and bit my lip, trying to stop myself from shaking and crying. I hadn't dreamed that nightmare in ages. Where it was coming from, why the demon came back I didn't know. I grabbed the satin sheet that covered me and pulled it over my shoulders, hoping it would warm me, not just outwardly, but inwardly. It didn't help. The arctic chill inside didn't melt by means of a sheet. I finally gave up and jumped off my bed, quickly slipping my robe on.

I won't remember this crap.

Every night, at least lately, it was the same old thing; the same old dream coming back to haunt me. It started again after the episode with Jacob and the redbone chick, and I'd be damned if I was going to keep allowing that, or a nighttime bogey man to keep me from sleeping. Having that decided, I pulled on my bunny slippers and walked quickly into the bathroom.

I brushed my teeth hard, ignoring the discomfort of the brush hitting against my sensitive gums. I was insistent on washing away the bad taste in my mouth that came not only from the typical morning breath, but also from the Freddie Kruger nightmare that had just visited me. After that, I pushed back the headband I used to control my hair and started my morning facial routine, then stepped into the shower. The warm water cascaded down my face and body, and finally I started feeling better, warmer. I started thinking about everything I still had to do to get ready for my evening dinner party. It was supposed to be a welcome Jacob back to the real world party, since for sure it's very hard to keep a grip on reality when you are undercover for a while.

Two hours later I had half of my meat platters made and had just finished washing my ham and getting it into the oven. Cooking was one gift I had inherited from my mother, or at least the love of it. I just didn't get to dally with the hobby as much as I would have liked.

The nerves that had been plaguing me since morning had calmed down some, but it didn't help when the doorbell suddenly rang. I knew it was Kendra. I was steamed with that girl. She was supposed to be here two hours earlier to help me cook. I rushed to the door, ready to do battle.

"Hey, girl!" she sang as I opened it.

I frowned. "About time you got here. You are only—" I looked down at my watch "—about two hours late."

"Well, don't fret, I'm here now." She was giddy, and bounced into my apartment, standing around as if she had been there all day.

I wasn't impressed.

"Mmm...what's that smell? I'm ready to chow down!"

"You were supposed to be here hours ago."

"I'm sorry, Kimberla. It's not like I was out getting my

hair done or something. I stopped by the office this morning and got hung up unexpectedly."

Kendra looked like she had just finished a shoot for *America's Next Top Model*. That was nothing unusual for her. She was casually decked out in a designer powder-blue jumpsuit and a pair of white, brand spanking new classic Lady Reeboks. Her newly permed hair was done up in a suave ponytail, showcasing her beautiful features perfectly. One thing that I admired about Kendra was regardless of her obvious beauty, the fact that she was intelligent could not be blurred. It was all over her. The way she walked, talked, moved her head. It all spoke volumes that Kendra Gray was far more than a pretty face. She was also a survivor. The loss of her husband and the graceful way she handled that loss, were a testimony, in my book, that many women could learn from.

I decided not to be mad at her, blaming her for my bad mood and morning.

"I really am sorry," Kendra said, as if she had just read my thoughts.

She flopped onto my couch. Then her attention seemed to go to my new rose-colored sofa and love seat. I had dark-gray pillows tossed across each one, my windows adorned by sheer pink curtains and matching ballooned valances.

"Too much pink, Kimberla," she decided.

I had already started toward the kitchen to grab a cold drink for us both. I walked back into the living room, smiling.

"Too much pink, huh?" I laughed. I really wasn't surprised at my friend's criticism of the new décor, in fact, I had expected it. Kendra had the flaw of a superiority complex. Only her dearest friends could tolerate it. But for some reason I found her confidence a lot like my own.

"Well..." Kendra raised her brow slightly as she looked around the room. "Not too much pink, just too much pink for you!"

I laughed. "I'm not even gonna fall into your insult ploy today. Got too much to do." I handed a smirking Kendra her Coke, opened my own, and walked back into the kitchen.

No matter how hard I tried to get into the laughing, joking comradery with Kendra that we normally had, that normally cheered me, I couldn't even smile without feeling it was fake, forced. I went to the kitchen sink and started washing the fresh pineapples in small squares for my fruit platter. I felt myself rinsing the same piece over and over again.

"Okay, guess what? I slept with my pastor last night."

"Huh?" I looked up. What on earth was Kendra talking about? "You did what?"

She laughed. "I just wanted to see how much you weren't paying attention to me. You haven't heard a word I've said." She patted the wooden stool next to the one she sat on, motioning me to sit beside her. "Come tell Dr. Feel Good what the problem is."

What was I supposed to say? Was I supposed to talk

about my nightmare? That would be bringing it to life. My mama always told me that anything that's in your head, keep it there, because the minute it flies out of your mouth you're giving it life and putting its energy into the universe. I decided to dodge that issue altogether and talk to my friend about things that girlfriends usually talk about, namely men.

"It's nothing," I finally said. I put the overwashed pineapple chunks in the bowl and walked over to Kendra, taking a seat on the stool. "Things have been kind of off between Jacob and me since he got back."

"I meant to ask you about him. You were so anxious to get him home." Kendra looked at me with concerned curiosity. "So how have things been off?"

"It's hard to pinpoint." I stopped speaking for a moment. I knew I needed to get my frustrations out, but truth was, I wasn't even sure what they were. "The sex is great."

"I just bet it is," Kendra said with a laugh. "But?"

I swear she knew me too well, probably better than I knew myself. I didn't answer her right away; instead I got up and started washing and paring fruit again.

"Kim, girl, you have to stop being so emotionally inverted," Kendra said quietly. She walked up beside me, leaning back against the counter. "You have this mask you put up, this tough girl self-image. But it doesn't work with me. I see through you."

"I'm not trying to mask anything," I said defensively.

"Yes, you are. You always do."

"You mean the same way you hide your feelings about Demetrius?" I said smartly.

Kendra's face suddenly changed, taking on a reddish hue. I immediately felt sorry. If there was one thing I hated about myself, it was my tendency to turn my pain and frustrations against anyone who tried to help me or who gave me uninvited advice, even if they meant well.

Kendra took a deep breath. "Demetrius has nothing to do with this," she whispered. "In fact, this is not about me or my late husband."

I didn't respond. I mean, what could I say? I couldn't talk about what was bothering me. That would require self admission. That would require facing my monster. I couldn't and wouldn't do that. Not now; maybe not ever.

I stayed quiet with my mental ramblings. I couldn't see, but I could feel Kendra's eyes on me.

"Okay," she said, realizing she was not going to get anything out of me, I supposed. "We have a lot of cooking to do." She looked around my somewhat messy kitchen. "And lots of cleaning to do."

By seven thirty that evening, everything was done and in place. You could smell the delicious aroma of my home-cooking just by passing by my condo window. I felt rather proud of myself, and Kendra, too. I had changed into a pair of dark blue jeans and matching vest. I strutted out of my bedroom, feeling rather pretty. That was unusual for me. Normally I would describe myself as femininely handsome.

By the time I waltzed into the living room my guests had started arriving. Kendra, being the social butterfly and lifesaver that she was, was greeting them as if she owned the place. A few of Jacob's good friends had arrived, Linda and Jerome, a married couple we'd had dinner with occasionally. I smiled a hello to them when the doorbell rang again, then rushed to answer it. I was somewhat disappointed when it was not Jacob.

"Well, damn, look at you!" Micah Latimer screamed. He walked in and took my hand.

I silently twirled around in a dancing circle.

"Don't I look chic in all my jeanie glory?" I teased.

"And to think I wanted her to wear an evening gown." Kendra walked up beside us. She reached her hand out to Micah. "I'm Kendra Gray."

"Micah, Micah Latimer. I didn't know Kimberla had friends as beautiful as she is."

I looked at Kendra's blushing and rolled my eyes. "I do believe your womanizing ways need a brushup, Micah."

We all laughed. Micah was still looking at Kendra with appreciation. Loving them both, I couldn't help but think that Micah was the type of man that could perhaps get Kendra out of the "no men allowed" slump she had been in since her husband's death. The wheels of matchmaker slowly started spinning in my head.

Two hours later Jacob still had not arrived. My evening had turned into an absolute mess. I didn't know if I was mad, scared, hurt, or all mixed together. Having everyone ask repeatedly where he was made it worse. It was his party! Everyone had already eaten and was enjoying cherry cheesecake, which Kendra had made.

I excused myself with a fake smile and exited to the bathroom. I doused my face with water for the second time, not even concerned with the fact that I had put a little makeup on.

After another three hours passed, people finally got tired of waiting for Jacob to show up and started leaving. I was so embarrassed but kept a frozen smile on my face, although I was fuming inside.

When everybody had left, I allowed my thoughts to drift to Jacob. *Where was he? Why did he do this?*

CHAPTER 6

Jacob

The night was as dark as it was long. I pulled up at Kimberla's place and took a deep breath. She had to be wondering why I hadn't called her all day. The fact is, I got tired of chasing her down with phone calls only to be told that she was busy, call back later. Or asking to see her, only to have her say she didn't feel like it. I told myself that I wasn't gonna press her. A brotha's got his pride. Was I being spiteful? I don't know.

I laughed at myself and turned off the ignition. If I was so "the man in charge," then why couldn't I stay away? Why couldn't I give her a day to miss me like I had told myself I would?

It was after 11:00 p.m., but Kimberla was more of a night owl, so it was surprising that her place was so dark. I gave her door three timid knocks. I knocked a couple more times. The door opened, but there was no one standing on the other side. I called out to her and walked inside.

"Kimmy? Where are you?"

Still not a sound. I looked around her living room and

saw her lying back on the couch, with a cigarette in her mouth. *What?*

"Damn," I said, "when did you start smoking?"

"None of your damn business."

"Huh?" That response set me back. "What on earth is your problem?"

She laughed, a crazy, half hysterical, half tearful laugh. The sound brought chills to my heart. Her laughing continued.

"Stop it, Kimmy!" I reached for her, to shake her, something. Something wasn't right with her.

I suddenly felt myself flying backward across the room. My head banged back against her bookshelf. Novels came flying off the shelves, one hitting me square on my forehead. When I looked up at Kimberla, she seemed as surprised as I was at her actions. What exactly she did, whatever karate move that sent me flying, I wasn't sure.

"Oh God!" she cried. "I can't—I can't do this!"

She stood with her hands over her eyes, shaking her head. I got up and quietly put the novels back on the bookshelf. I then walked over and past her, sat on the couch and waited. After a few more minutes rolled by, and she still stood there with her face covered, I spoke up.

"So you wanna tell me what this is all about?" I was almost scared to walk up to her, to touch her.

"I don't think I can take this anymore, Jacob," she whispered.

"Take what?"

She finally turned around, looking at me with an incredulous expression. "How could you sit there like you don't know? Jacob, I've been trying to call you all night and you wouldn't even answer the phone! You know I had your party tonight, and you didn't even respect me enough to show up!"

"No way! You told me it was tomorrow, Kimmy. I specifically remember you saying the—"

"I specifically told you the seventh, and today is Friday, the seventh!"

I thought back for a moment, mostly picturing a mental calendar of the day of the week versus the date. I felt a sickening "oh no!" feeling hitting my gut.

"I'm sorry, babe. I really got the dates mixed up." I got up and reached out to her with my arms spread. "You know I would never have just not come."

She put her hands up, as if to ward me off. "You know what? It's not even so much that you didn't show up. Although I had a houseful of people and spent all day cooking and preparing, only to be made a fool of when everyone knew it was for you and you did a no-show. It's the fact that you didn't even call or make any attempt to talk to me the whole day. It's the fact that nobody is gonna take care of me and how I feel but me. I can't do this…"

"You can't do what? And I know I didn't call." I sighed. "But, Kimmy, you've been acting like you really were still trippin' about Lolita, and every time I called you there was some push-back excuse as to why you didn't want to or couldn't spend some time together."

"So you purposely didn't call? Didn't answer your cell phone?"

I knew the guilt had to be written all over my face. It had to be, because I felt it all over my body. "I didn't call. As for my not answering my cell phone, I left it at home earlier this evening and I didn't go back to get it once I was out. I didn't want to be looking at it all night, hoping and waiting for you to call."

"Who were you with? That woman?"

"No, I wasn't with Lo-Lo! I just had some 'me' time."

This time when I put my arms around her, she didn't push them away. I thought that was a good sign of her softening up, until...

"You know, Jacob, maybe you do need some *you* time. That sounds really healthy. I need the same thing. I think we should take some time away from each other."

"That's not how you work out disagreements, Kimberla."

"I don't want to work out anything."

"But I do. Baby, please."

"But I don't. And, Jacob, will you please, please leave?"

I put my arms down. Somehow what she was trying to say to me wasn't coming through clearly. Maybe I didn't want it to come through.

"Okay, I will. Can I call you tomorrow?" I asked her.

"No. Let's just leave it like this. I need to focus on this

case, and we need to figure out where we are. I really don't have any time to complicate things with a man in my life and—"

That hurt. "A man in your life? So that's all I am to you? I'm just another man in your life for you to dismiss? Forget the fact that I'm in love with you?"

"Please leave."

"I love you." My voice cracked on the word *love*. Funny thing is, I knew that Kimberla wasn't where I was in this relationship, on the same page. But I never thought she would be doing what she was trying to do. I didn't want to think it now, either. My head started throbbing.

Kimberla took a deep breath and walked over to the front door. She opened it and turned toward me. Even now, there were no tears coming down her face, although her eyes were bright and glassy. *Did she not care for me at all?*

"You don't love me at all, Kimmy?"

She wrapped her hands around her arms. "Believe it or not, Jacob, it's really not about you. It's not about us. It's about me. I'm not ready to give you what you need."

"But?"

"Shhh…" she said, covering my mouth with her two fingers. "Give me some time, please. Just leave, please."

Somehow, minutes later, I found myself standing on the other side of the door, having just lost the woman who held my heart. And the most painful thing about it was I didn't even know why.

* * *

Catwomyn75

She walked into her apartment and slammed the door. She was pissed. None of them were worth the breath they breathed. No good, trifling-ass men. None of them deserved to live! Selfish, that's all they were, selfish animals; God's mistake!

She threw her keys onto the coffee table and looked around, fighting to get her equilibrium back, but it wasn't working. She walked over to her wet bar and poured a brandy. It felt tingly and warm going down her throat. It eased her ache, but not her anger, her burning righteous anger.

In anger she tossed the crystal brandy glass across the darkened room, splattering it against the wall. The noise made her laugh. She fell against the sofa, still laughing, harder and harder till tears rolled down her cheeks. She saw the faces of the men, all of them lusting for her. That last look on their faces when they realized something wasn't quite right. It was exhilarating, thrilling. And she didn't want to stop.

She got up slowly from the couch; her laughter still rang in her ears. She walked into her bedroom, flicked on the light, and spotted his picture on the side table. She picked it up. He was handsome. His smile was wicked as if he knew. He knew what a cheat he was. He knew that even as he posed for the picture she snapped, he was posing for the homosexual men he was meeting at the all-male peek shows he frequented.

She picked up a sharp letter holder that was resting on her desk, and then pulled the photo out of its frame. Laying the glass covering softly on her desk, she placed the photo on top of it. Her hand started swinging, back and forth, ripping at his cheeks, his eyes, his nose, trying to rip out his soul.

By the time she stopped swinging, blood and broken glass from the frame were splattered on the desk. She looked at the blood that dripped down her fingers.

She tasted it and smiled.

CHAPTER 7

Kimberla

Micah was late, as always. I struggled to find a decent R&B station while waiting in my car. My day had seemed to drag by. Maybe it was because it had been the first day of my so-called single status. In all honesty, Jacob and I hadn't been seeing each other for that long, but Jacob was not a low-key man by any means. He was strong, vibrant, full of energy. He had integrity and was an honorable man. But he was also fun, sexy, and intelligent, which made him a GAM, an all-around good-ass man.

I watched a hummingbird flapping its wings against the sweet leaves of a rosebush. That reminded me of something else that had to be added to his GAM resume. Jacob was sweet, like that bush, so why couldn't I be like that bird, and give him what he so dearly wanted? Why couldn't I trust it? So much of my inner being wasn't making a lot of sense to me lately. Like those dreams… Where they were coming from, what they meant, why I couldn't shake this foreboding feeling of familiarity with the face in my dreams, I didn't know. But I did know it was destroying my peace and the ability to perform my job. It had already destroyed my relationship. Something had to give, but what? My nightmare was turning into my day-mare.

I swallowed hard. My mouth was so dry. At the present, all I could think about was something cold, like a Dr Pepper. And where on earth was Micah?

An abrupt knock on my car window made me jump. That was something else that was new, off, and just not right. I never jumped in nervousness. My study of martial arts taught me that. The vitalness of total calm was something I had learned was key in making sure that the element of surprise was never your foe, but instead your strength. I had to get my mind together.

"Scared you, huh?" Micah said. He ran around to the passenger door and hopped inside.

"Whatever."

Micah laughed.

"Okay, Kimberla. So what happened last night? Did Jacob ever show up?"

I knew he was gonna ask that. I tried to keep my facial expression blank. The last thing I needed was someone delving into my thoughts. I was having enough trouble trying to figure them out on my own.

"No, he never showed up. It was a misunderstanding of the time and dates."

"Yeah, right. And you believed that?" Micah said, choking back a sigh. "I need to talk to my boy. He's making the rest of us brothas look bad with that sorry, lame excuse."

"Micah, I really don't want to talk about it anymore, okay?"

I paused at the stoplight. I tried to catch my breath, taking deep ones to steady myself. It wasn't working.

"What's wrong?" Micah asked in concern. "Did you two argue last night?"

"Micah, let it go! I'm just worried about this case and us not coming up with a damn thing!"

"Whoa!" he exclaimed. "Okay, so let's talk about the case. I was looking over the records and some of the evidence. I don't know about you, but I'm starting to smell serial killer with a strong funk."

"Ugh! Now why is this suddenly a serial killing? And if you think that's what it is, why are we going to scope out this club?" *Why was I feeling so irritated?*

Micah looked at me, perplexed. I didn't much blame him. I could feel myself tittering on the edge of a blowout.

"For one thing, Kimberla, this was Kyte's idea, as you know. And if you stop tripping for a minute and think about what I just said, I questioned if this *could* be a serial case, I didn't say it *was*. I said it's starting to *smell* like one."

I cringed, not at Micah's tone but my own. I knew why we were going to the club. Babatunde, the name of the club, was the last place Kaseem Soroco had been spotted. Kyte felt that we could nose around a bit, ask a few curious questions, and maybe find out what Soroco had been involved in and who would want to kill him.

I decided to stop acting bitchy and put my personal issues aside for Micah's sake. At least for now.

He pointed to a parking spot on the other side of the street from the club. The street was flooded with island folks and African natives. I took a quick survey of our surroundings, making sure we were legally parked. We didn't want to make ourselves seem too noticeable. I took my compact out of my purse and gave my lightly made up face a once-over.

"Okay," I said, "let's see how the Africans roll."

The music was wild and the crowd, surprisingly, was sedate and calm. Micah grabbed my hand and walked in. His head bobbed casually to the music as a young, chocolate-brown Nigerian man led us to our table.

"This is different," I said. I picked up the paper menu that was stationed between the salt and pepper shakers, and gave it a quick look-over.

"I don't want to waste too much time in here," Micah said.

"Why not? You're among your peoples." I laughed.

He gave me an "I'm gonna cut you" look. I always picked on Micah about his African black complexion. I supposed Kyte thought we could pass for natives as long as Micah could give a great fake accent and be convincing.

"You can tease all you want. Women love this dark berry. Take one look at me and they know I got one of those extra-long mojos, you know what I mean?"

"Um-hmm…and you do know, if women believe you're Nigerian they will also think the rest of the fable is true."

"What fable?"

"You know, that African men are sexually selfish and restrained and don't give oral. Here in the States you won't get no booty if you don't—" I stuck my tongue out and flicked it "—lick da booty."

"Kimberla!" Micah screamed in shock. "I can't believe you!"

I giggled naughtily. Our waiter showed up in the midst of our teasing chatter. It felt good to laugh with Micah again. Although deep down I was still feeling a bit on the dark side; inside, laughing seemed to be a temporary fix.

Micah started chatting with the waiter as we gave our order, but I was a bit surprised when he bluntly said to him, "It was a terrible thing what happened to that dude, what was his name? Soroco? You didn't know him, did you?"

I was even more surprised when our waiter seemed more than happy to talk about it. Micah winked at me. I guess he knew what he was doing. And I couldn't help but look at him with admiration.

Jacob

Love is sexiest. There is always some word of compassion or advice for ladies with broken hearts, always some love song they can listen to about waiting to exhale or whatever they need to make the hurt feel better. Always some movie that tells their story and empathizes. But men? We have to struggle on our own. Back in the day there were the crooner songs, "Make Up To Break Up,"

"Thin Line Between Love And Hate," we had all those. But that was old school. Nowadays the rappers have taken over the so-called masculine mentality of the black male. Nowadays all you hear is if your lady doesn't love ya, forget her, go find another bed warmer, or better yet, go make more money and laugh in her face. What about the men who don't want another, like me?

My mind was mush. I sat in a downtown Baltimore bar trying to figure out where I went wrong. I could see if I had actually done something. Cheated, flirted, ignored her, or failed to please her in the bedroom department, but the last time I checked, her multiples were coming on the regular, unless she was faking it. I wasn't that out of sync, was I?

"Ready for another one?" the heavyset Caucasian bartender asked me, nodding toward my empty glass.

"Yeah," I whispered, "but this time, make it vodka, straight. Shit, make it a double."

His eyebrows rose. "You sure you want to mix your liquor like that? You aren't driving, are you?"

"Man, do you want my money or not?"

He bobbed his shoulders and went to fix my drink. I took a deep breath, allowing my thoughts to swing back to Kimberla. I couldn't help but wonder what she was doing, if she was thinking about me, missing me at all. Probably not.

I spent the next hour washing my liver in vodka, trying to ease my pain away. I hadn't planned on falling in love with Kimberla. It just happened. And although I knew from the start she was not going to be an easy woman to deal with, I never knew a woman who didn't want to be loved, who had some abhorrence to it. I closed my eyes, feeling a buzz coming over me. I wished I could get some answers. Oddly enough I wished I could talk to my late wife about this. She had been my best friend, and even though she was gone, I knew she would want me to be happy. Sometimes we need an angel on our shoulder to direct us, even if it's one that used to share our life.

"You know that you won't find the answer in a bottle, right?"

I turned to the voice that was echoing in my ear. My eyes had to focus, and for a moment I thought I was seeing my late wife Regina's ghost. I blinked. It wasn't her, but it was a beautiful woman, smiling sweetly at me.

"So why don't you put that down," she continued, "and let me buy you some coffee?"

"Uh, no, I don't need any coffee."

She turned around backward on her stool so that she was facing me. Her eyes were glued on mine.

"Look, baby, I'm not in the mood for a pickup tonight," I slurred. "You're pretty enough for plenty of brothas up in here to be more than willing. No insult meant."

"Wow!" She laughed. Her long blond braid flew over her right shoulder and her blue eyes sparkled.

Not bad, I thought, if she was my type, or if I could get one tall, cocoa-colored FBI beauty out of my mind.

"I'm not trying to pick you up. I'm just trying to comfort you."

I gulped down the last of my drink and nodded to the bartender to fill it up again.

"I hope you're catching a cab home, because if you're driving you could risk this man losing his liquor license," the blond woman said. The bartender refilled my glass, but nodded in agreement with her.

I looked from one to the other. "Okay, I'm catching a cab, all right? Why y'all up in my damn business?" I looked over to the woman. "Do I look like I need comforting?"

"You look like your whole world is falling apart," she said quietly. "And the only reason a handsome man like you would be in a place like this drinking himself into a coma is either, one, he just lost his job, or two, love trouble."

I felt even more amusement washing over me. The last thing I was gonna do was sit in a bar talking to some strange woman about my love life. I shook my head, downed my latest shot of vodka, and looked up to tell her about herself so that she would get lost. I paused. Right behind her I saw a familiar face, one I hadn't seen in over a year, and one I thought I would never see again. My face must have reflected my shock.

"Are you okay?" the woman said.

I had closed my eyes, and then opened them again slowly, thinking the image would disappear. It didn't. The person looked at me with a sinister grin, then started walking away. I jumped up to follow him, knocking my stool to the floor as I stood. The loud clanging sound brought all eyes to me, but I didn't care. I made my move to follow him. Damn the vodka, I thought, as I stumbled.

"Hold up!" the bartender said. "You haven't paid your tab yet!"

I hastily threw a twenty on the counter, not bothering to wait for the change. The shadowy figure was moving quickly. Too quickly for me and my drunk, clumsy ass.

"Hold up!" I screamed out, startling the crowd.

The person kept running, disappearing out the side door of the bar. I followed. A light mist of rain had begun to come down, making the sidewalk somewhat slippery. I supposed my Timberland boots didn't appreciate the punishment, 'cause I soon found myself facedown and kissing the wet sidewalk, but not before I got a better view of the person I was chasing.

No matter how much vodka I had consumed, no one would ever be able to tell me there wasn't life after death. I would swear on everything holy that I had just chased former FBI agent Malcolm Johnson.

CHAPTER 8

Kimberla

By the time we had eaten our dinner and Micah had finished his nosey yet clever interviews with some of the Babatunde patrons, it had started raining outside. We rushed to the car, with him politely opening my door for me. I smiled at his fake play of chivalry.

"So do you open the door for all your dates, Mr. Latimer?"

"I'm just showing you how a real man treats his woman," he said teasingly.

I had to admit Micah was cute with his chocolate self and shiny white teeth. Why he couldn't seem to keep a woman around was beyond my imagination. Could have something to do with his noncommittal ways, but then again, wasn't I having trouble committing in my own relationship? Um...let me restate. I had trouble committing in my old relationship, being that Jacob and I were no more.

"Hmph," I teased. "So you're supposed to be a real man, huh? Is that why you're single every other month?"

"It's not me," he protested. "It's those damn women!"

"Uh-huh."

Micah closed the door and stuck his head through the passenger-side window. "Well, I will tell you this much. When I do find the woman that I love and completes me, I'm gonna marry her. What about you?"

"Micah, um…women are not my cup of tea, okay? I don't roll like that. So I don't think I'll be marrying one any time soon."

"Cute," he said with a chuckle. He was resting his elbows on my window edge.

"Are you gonna just stand there gawking at me or are we leaving sometime soon? Besides, we need to call Kyte and let him in on the big fat nothings we came up with tonight."

"Not until you answer a question."

"What question?"

"When you are in love, and I already know you are, when are you gonna stop being foolish and marry Jacob? Or at least forgive him for whatever the hell he was supposed to have done?"

I felt myself getting hot inside. I swear Micah never quits. My lips had parted to respond to him when I suddenly heard a popping sound. Micah's mouth opened as if he was about to speak. Instead, blood poured out. His eyes stared into mine before he flopped face-forward over me. His blood poured into my lap.

"Micah!" I screamed.

Another shot rang out. I then noticed the perpetrator pulling at my door handle and pointing his gun at my face.

Even with my panic over Micah, my agent instincts immediately kicked in. I decided to help the shooter out. As he was pulling at the door I opened it, pushing hard against the frame. He flew backward, stumbling and almost falling to the ground. I rushed out of the car, quickly grabbing my gun from my ankle holster. The unknown man and I wrestled in the street. I fought to disarm him and at the same time, dropped my own gun.

The man was short, but he made up for that with his tremendous girth, and he was sure to use that weight against me. He grabbed my head with one hand. It covered my neck and he started banging my head hard against the graveled street. I was getting dizzy and pain was shooting through my skull. Tears shot to my eyes, but I was determined not to let them fall. With his weapon in between us, I was sure I was about to take a bullet, but I managed to hold tight to it. A loud sound exploded, the sound of a gun firing. Both of us lay completely still, neither of us being sure who had been shot, him or me. I felt pain all over my body and then I slowly felt myself losing consciousness, until a deep dark blackness enveloped me.

Jacob

I wasn't drunk, I told myself. I was just dizzy and tired and freakin' depressed. But that wasn't gonna stop me from taking my butt home so I could sleep. My thoughts were all over the place. I kept seeing images of who I thought was Malcolm Johnson, and then they would swing back to Kimberla's words, that we needed time apart, and then back to former FBI agent Johnson. Maybe I was imagining what I saw. That sucka was dead. Wasn't he?

After I left the bar I decided to make my way home. The rain didn't make my vision any easier. I pulled out of the parking lot quickly, pushing on the brakes as my wheels began to spin in place. I laughed. I guess that was my cue to slow down. I drove down the street, and I felt like I was going in slow motion. My windshield wiper blades swung back and forth like limp tree leaves.

I was feeling nice, if you want to call it that, but I didn't realize how nice until ten minutes later. The roar of police sirens had me on alert in a second.

"Shit!" I said out loud. I opened my glove compartment, took out some mint breath freshener, and gave myself a few squirts. I didn't want my breath smelling like gin and OJ. I was clearing my throat when there was a loud tap on my car window. I rolled it down.

"What's the problem, Officer?" I asked with an innocent smile.

"Can I see your driver's license and registration, please?"

"Sure—sure..." I fiddled with my wallet, and then handed him my credentials, including my FBI badge. "I wasn't going too fast, was I?"

The officer paused for a minute. *Crap,* I thought. *This is the last thing I need.*

"Well, who would have thought? Jacob White?"

I squinted to see exactly who this officer was, who obviously knew me by name. Or at least knew of me.

"What are you doing racing down the street like a bat out of hell in this weather?" he asked. "Kind of reckless, too. Have you been drinking?"

"Derek?"

I knew this cat. I guess luck was my partner tonight. I smirked, and got out of my car. Derek Ivy had been on the training committee almost ten years ago, back when I was a young, proud, Maryland State Trooper. He was one of the few Caucasian officers willing to help me get used to the difficult transition between city officer and state trooper. The truth was that a lot of the white officers resented the affirmative action quotas that gave some of the black officers the break of instant hire. At least quicker than white officers.

I didn't include myself in that group. As far as I was concerned I worked my ass off to get where I had gotten, and didn't owe anyone a thank-you or an apology. Derek had been one of the few white men who agreed with my reasoning, and had had my back more than once.

He gave me a bear hug. "How've you been, man?"

"I've been good. Just working and living. You know they be killing me in D.C.!"

"I bet they do. Y'all steal any big cases lately?" He flicked my FBI badge at me.

"Yeah, you're funny."

It was great seeing him again. But I knew what he was

talking about. It was no secret that local and state authorities felt that the FEDS were famous for sticking their noses and badges in cases where they didn't belong.

"I'm just mad tired, man. I just came back a week ago. Working an undercover gig in Chitown."

I yawned and leaned back against my vehicle. The rain had stopped and the cool summer air felt kind of good.

"So, what are you doing out tonight?" he asked.

"Just relaxing, chillaxing, enjoy my time off—"

"Drinking," Derek cut in.

"I said relaxing." I reached my hand out casually for my license and badge. "But right now I just want to get home and get some sleep."

Surprisingly, Derek held my ID up in the air over his head. He laughed. "Um, Jacob, just because I know your ass doesn't mean I'm letting you get away with swerving all over the road and speeding. Exactly how much have you had to drink? And don't try to tell me you're totally sober. You should know me and my instincts better than that."

"Awww, man. Don't do it, Derek! Come on now. Don't do this to me!" I gave him a pained expression.

"*How* much?"

"A few, a'ight?" I groaned when Derek started shaking his head. "Look, I promise I'll drive straight home. I just need some sleep man, and I'm five minutes away."

"I can't let you do it, my friend."

I sighed, and then put both hands out in a cuffed position.

Derek laughed. "I'm not trying to arrest you, man, I'm just gonna drive you home. Don't worry, I'll make sure your car makes it home behind you."

He chuckled at the drop-dead look I gave him.

"Honestly," he said, "I'm doing you a favor."

I supposed he was right. Anyone else would have been getting a ride to lockup. Not a ride home. After we had gotten in his vehicle, I closed my eyes and leaned back. I started feeling the beginnings of a massive headache. Vodka always had this negative affect on me. I started drifting off, but I could hear Derek talking to me. I just couldn't make out what he was saying.

"What did you say?" I asked him.

"I said I'm surprised that you were out drinking, with all that's been going on tonight with your agents."

I opened my tired eyes at his words. "What do you mean all that's been going on?"

"You haven't heard? Jacob, they found two of your people, two federal agents, gunned down at this African club in southeast D.C. A male and a female agent."

I inhaled in shock; my heart melted, and the only word that managed to fly, or rather scream, its way past my lips was "Kimberla!"

CHAPTER 9

Jacob

I jumped out of the car almost before Derek put his foot on the brakes to park. All I could think about was getting to the emergency room and making sure it wasn't Kimberla lying on a hospital cot, hurt or, much worse, dead.

"Hold up, man!" Derek called out.

I ignored him, then tripped over the sidewalk curb, almost falling flat on my face. I fought to keep my balance and raced inside the automatic doors of Holy Cross Hospital. I pushed my way into the emergency room past some poor, sick old man who was coughing. But I didn't have time to be polite.

God, just let her be okay, I prayed. Just let her be okay....

Unsurprisingly, the emergency waiting room was full of federal agents, including Kyte Williams. I was fine with seeing him, being that he headed the D.C. division. He would have to show up no matter who it was that had gotten hit. But when I looked around to my right, I saw some people that I didn't wish to see. Kimberla's dad and stepmom were sitting together holding hands. Mr. Bacon looked totally shaken. All my hopes were dashed at that moment. I knew it was her.

"Mr. Bacon…"

Kimberla's father looked at me. Tears coated his eyes.

"Jacob," he said plainly. He walked over and grabbed me in his typical, signature bear hug.

I hugged him back, and reached next to him and gave his wife a slight kiss on the cheek. Looking back to Mr. Bacon, I hesitated to ask, but I had to know. "Is she?"

"She's okay," he said. He nodded toward the examination rooms. "She's in there."

I took a deep breath and had started walking in that direction when I was suddenly stopped.

"Jacob."

I turned around to see Kyte Williams's tired face. "I need to talk to you before you see Kim," he said.

"What happened to her?"

"We're not even sure, Jacob. All I know is I have one agent dead, and another with a severe concussion. And no idea who, what, or why." Kyte sighed in frustration. "I'm worried that either someone leaked information about the case Latimer and Kimberla were working on or they weren't careful enough at the club. And I don't want to believe either of those notions."

I felt a slight rise in my temperature and the need to defend Kimberla. I lowered my voice, so that Kimberla's dad wouldn't hear me, and whispered, "You know what type of agent Kimberla is. She is always careful. So please don't even try that last guess."

"Jacob, you know what I'm saying."

I switched subjects quickly. "What happened to Micah?"

"He was shot in the head. It seemed almost like an execution." Kyte was rubbing his temples as he spoke. "All I know is we are gonna find out who did this. I have every source available on the job."

I cringed at Kyte's words. Shot in the head... Micah was a great guy, and he didn't deserve to go out like that. But regardless, I couldn't help but feel relieved that it hadn't been Kimberla.

"I need to see Kimberla," I said to Kyte.

"Of course you do." He touched my arm as I started to walk away.

"But listen, Jacob. I am seriously thinking about making her go on a long, long vacation, and putting some other agents on the case she was working on. I want to talk to you about it to see if you're up to it. I know that you've worked with Lolita in Los Angeles, and I'm definitely thinking about pulling her into things. She's an excellent agent. Maybe you can hint to Kimberla that she needs some rest. You know how stubborn she is, so it's not gonna be easy to convince her. Plus, she's pretty shaken up about Latimer, so be prepared, okay?"

"I don't know if I'm the one to hint anything to Kimberla, Kyte."

"Just try? Or at least see where you think her mind is and report back to me, okay?"

I nodded, and swallowed deep inside. I wasn't only worried about Kimberla's mental state over Micah. I was also worried that she wouldn't want to see me.

Kimberla

Have you ever known that you were awake, but the agony of consciousness was so painful that you willed yourself to sleep?

I kept my eyes closed while lying motionless in the cool, sterile hospital room. Every time I even thought to move, I felt pain. It wasn't so much the pain from my injuries, which were actually minor; it was the pain from what had happened to Micah. The knock upside my head hadn't done a thing to my memory, or the vivid picture in my mind that played over and over again like a horror flick. I cried inside and pulled my sheet and blanket closer to my chin. Still I didn't open my eyes. I couldn't figure out what was happening, why so many bad things were going on in my life for the past few years, why my bad dreams had come back, but mostly why I wasn't enjoying my work as I used to. For the first time, thoughts of a different occupation were very real to me. But I knew that before I even entertained that notion, I had to find out who attacked me, and who killed Micah, and why.

I heard the door crack open and someone walk in, then felt a hand touch my arm through the covers. I still didn't open my eyes, but I didn't have to. I knew it was Jacob. I felt my throat tighten.

"Kimmy," he whispered.

I was quiet, yet I could feel my lips quivering.

"I know you're awake, and I know you hear me. Girl, what have you gotten yourself into? You're famous for scaring me to death!"

"Micah's dead," I stated flatly.

"I know." Jacob touched my face.

Until then I had been able to hold it together, but at the feel of his strong yet tender touch, the dam broke loose. A slow tear trickled down my cheek.

"Open your eyes, baby."

His words made even more tears fall. I opened my eyes slowly, then licked my lips, tasting my own tears. "I'm fine."

"No, you're not fine," Jacob insisted.

He reached up to wipe the moisture from beneath my eyes. Instantly I turned away. Jacob didn't comment on that. I jumped at the squeaky sound of him pulling a chair close to my bed.

"So what happened tonight?" he asked. "Do you feel like talking about it?"

"We went to check out the club. We were undercover, of course, but everything went smooth. I honestly don't know what happened."

Jacob had a puzzled look on his face. "Do you think someone in the club suspected you two of being agents?"

"Jacob, please! I'm not some amateur and neither is—was Micah."

I sighed. A sharp pain struck me at the right of my temple. "I want to get some rest please," I said sadly.

"Of course."

It was quiet for a moment. Obviously neither one of us could think of anything to say.

"Baby, you should let Kyte put someone else on this case. I'm worried about you, and since we don't know who is responsible for this attack, I think it would be smart to let it go."

I didn't even respond to that. But I could feel my temperature rising, even with my headache roaring on.

"I don't want to talk about it, Jacob."

"Kim—"

"I said I don't want to talk about it!" I screamed.

I turned my head away from Jacob. I swallowed hard, trying not to cry. Somehow I was going to find out who killed Micah. I was also going to solve the Soroco murder case. I wasn't going to give up. Giving up was not even a part of who I was, and if Kyte or Jacob couldn't understand that, then neither of them could understand me, either.

A mental picture of Micah came to my mind, and the tears started to fall. This time I didn't even bother to stop them.

CHAPTER 10

Kimberla

The following few days passed by quickly. I don't know if it was because of the number of visitors that I had at the hospital, or because of the place my own mentality had put me. I felt like I owed Micah so much, and I couldn't think of anything else. I owed it to him to find his killer. That meant also solving the murder case that we had worked so hard on together. So in the midst of my healing, there was my busy little mind, working overtime to figure it all out.

I had spent three days in the hospital, and was anxious to get home. My so-called rest wasn't as restful as it should've been, either. Kyte Williams and Jacob were almost dogmatic about me giving my case over to someone else. But that wasn't how I operated. I wasn't a quitter, and both of them knew it.

My mind was busy and filled with plans that I hadn't quite organized yet. I had spent three days in the hospital and was anxious to get home. Riding there with my friend Kendra at the wheel wasn't as relaxing as it should have been, and she seemed to be able to read my mood.

"Are you okay?" she asked.

I smiled weakly at her. "Yes. I'm just anxious, and tired, too, I guess."

"Well, you should be, sis." She squeezed my arm as if to comfort me. "You've been through a helluva lot."

She pulled up at my complex and shut off the engine. It purred down with a squeaky sound.

"You need a tune-up, Kendra."

"Jiffy Lube?"

"Yeah." We both laughed. Pain shot through my head and I cringed.

"You aren't in any pain, are you?" Kendra quizzed with concern.

"Not really. You know, I was mostly bruised up. But my head got the biggest bang. What I need is to get my butt back to work."

Kendra looked skeptical. "I don't know about that. But listen, you go on in the house and I'll get your bags, okay?"

"Thanks, sweetie," I said, smiling at her gratefully.

I walked to my door, glad to be home but feeling conscious of my surroundings. There was no guarantee that the person that planned the attack on me, and that murdered Micah, was the same man I fought with, the man that was now deceased. Jacob and Kyte continually reminded me of that. Not that I would be fool enough not to realize it myself. I just needed to use my third eye from now on.

I was opening my front door slowly and could hear Kendra coming behind me with my bags.

"Oh my God!" I cried, once I had opened the door.

"What's wrong?" Kendra asked, rushing up beside me.

I was speechless. Wall-to-wall bright red roses filled my living room. They were the most beautiful arrangements I had ever seen. Not that I had seen many. And I definitely wasn't the type of woman who received them often, either.

I knew immediately who had done this, and tears filled my eyes at the thought of him.

"Aw, Kimberla, they are beautiful!" Kendra exclaimed. She took the card from my coffee table and opened it, since I was too stunned to move. She read the card.

"Just something to make your homecoming a little sweeter. And to let you know that I love you, and I'm thinking about you. Always, Jacob."

"Wow!"

My mind and heart echoed Kendra's sentiments. Why, why, why did Jacob have to do something so sweet? Why did he have to leave me so confused? And the biggest question, why did I end things with him in the first place?

"Do you love him?"

I looked at Kendra, juggling with her question in my mind. "Love doesn't always fix things, girl."

She sighed. "So you do love him?"

"What difference does it make, Kendra? I can't be with him right now!"

"Why?"

My lips trembled as I spoke. "Just leave it alone, okay?"

"So you do love him," Kendra pressed.

"As I told you before, love doesn't always fix things. You should know this yourself. I mean, you loved Demetrius, but did that fix the problems you two had?"

Kendra looked at me as if I had slapped her. To be honest I wished I could slap myself.

Pain filled her eyes as she stood up. "This has nothing to do with Demetrius. Absolutely nothing. I was talking about you. But hey, you deal with your relationship. I'm gonna get you unpacked."

She grabbed my bags and headed to my bedroom. And I sat around my rose-filled living room, feeling like an absolute ass.

Jacob

I gave Kimberla's front door a timid knock. I honestly couldn't take waiting any longer to see her reaction or how she felt about the roses I had sent her. To be honest I wasn't normally a super mushy type of man, and Kimberla pretty much knew this about me. If she couldn't see how much I loved her now, she never would. I was starting to feel like some desperate puppy.

She opened the door on my third knock, and there we both stood, staring at each other and neither of us saying anything. Her eyes told me that she knew I would show up before the day was over, and had been expecting me.

"Kendra brought you home?"

"Yes."

I stepped inside, uninvited, and looked around to see if she was alone. "She still here?" I asked.

Kimberla stepped back. "She left two hours ago," she said nervously.

"I'm not gonna bite you, baby."

I looked down at her full, succulent lips, wanting so badly to kiss them.

"What are you trying to do, Jacob? Why are you here? Why the roses? Why?"

"You don't like them?"

"I love them! But—"

"I'm trying to get you to see how crazy this is," I said, reaching my hand out and caressing her cheek. "We don't need a break from each other. You just need to tell me what's bothering you. I mean, I know you're upset about Micah, but what's this break, and why?"

I could tell I was making her uncomfortable. I just couldn't back down. There had been only two women in my life that I could honestly say I'd loved. Losing one of them was beyond my control; I wasn't gonna lose Kimberla without a fight.

"Jacob, let's not do this."

"Do what?"

She shook her head vehemently. My heart dropped. Something inside me was telling me I was making a fool of myself, yet something else was telling me to hold on. The latter voice was starting to become louder.

I sighed deeply. "I guess I'd better leave."

I didn't leave right away, though. I stood there for a minute, as if expecting her to say, *don't go!* What the hell was the matter with me?

I had made a military about-face turn to her door to leave when I finally heard the words I'd been waiting to hear.

"Jacob, wait."

I exhaled and faced her again.

"I don't know what's wrong," she said with a shaky voice. "I don't wanna be alone. I haven't been feeling myself for a long time. I've been feeling confused and now this horror with Micah and—and—"

I didn't let her finish, I grabbed her in my arms and covered her lips with mine. She didn't pull away. Her willingness hardened my body. I pulled her close to me and softly sucked her tongue into my mouth.

"Mmm...Jacob."

"Come on," I whispered, leading her step by step into her bedroom.

We stood in front of her bed, and I could almost see her shaking. I didn't know or understand where her head was, or what was going on with her, but at this point I was just content with the knowledge that I didn't leave her cold. It was pretty obvious from the fire in her eyes, fire that mirrored the heat in my own, that she was nowhere near cold.

I put my arms around her waist, held her, and looked deep into her eyes.

"Do you want me?" I asked, almost begging. "Or do you want to talk?"

Kimberla closed her eyes and wrapped her arms around my neck. She buried her face against it. "Just take me away. I don't wanna think right now. Just make me forget everything. Just for a little while…"

She didn't have to say any more. I stood for a moment and just stared at her. I almost laughed, thinking about what my dad used to say when he was giving me one of his heart-to-heart talks about women and love. *When you find a woman that you only have to look at and feel content, you're whipped, boy, straight-up whipped.*

I pushed Kimberla onto the bed and then pulled her to the edge of it. I took her bare feet in my hands and began to caress them. I looked at her seductively and then slowly began to suck on her toes, one by one. She took a deep breath. I sucked her big toe into my mouth as if I were suckling the warmth between her legs. That would come later. Encouraged by her sighs, I moved to the balls of her feet, then to her ankles, her calves, leaving a trail of wetness as I went.

She moaned; I moaned. I reached her inner thigh and stopped. I just wanted to worship this woman. I wanted to show her with my every touch how much I loved and needed her. But I wanted her to want and need me, too. I needed reassurance that had been lost by her saying that we needed a break. To me those words said she didn't want me anymore, and I needed to really know she did.

By the time I reached her midsection, Kimberla was panting and moaning my name. I held her slim hips and tight, round ass in the palm of one of my hands, steadying her. I flattened my tongue and licked her, slowly, from her vagina opening to her clit.

"Ohhhhhhhhhhh!" she moaned, arching up against my tongue.

I used my free hand to loosen my belt buckle. Her taste was intoxicating me. With her quivering thighs clinging to my shoulders, I licked and sucked and strummed her love button like a violin. I moved downward and dipped inside her again and again. She was shaking, calling my name in a sexual frenzy.

"Don't stop," she cried. "Please—please…"

Despite her pleas, I did stop. I couldn't wait any longer. I had to be inside her.

I moved up over her wet, aroused body. "Say you want me."

"I want you."

"Mmm…" I moaned, rubbing the tip of my dick around her clit. "Say you need me, baby."

Her head swung from side to side. "I need you, God, please!"

I wanted and needed something more from her. I had to hear it. I grabbed her chin with my hand, forcing her to look at me. I was poised to enter her but I didn't, not yet. I wanted her to beg for it. I wanted her to say…

"Say you love me, Kimmy."

"I— Oh, Jacob!"

"Say it."

"Please, stop teasing me."

I still didn't give her what she wanted. What I knew she craved, although I could barely contain myself. I needed to hear the words!

"Say it, baby. Tell me you're in love with me."

"Oh! Oh! I love you, Jacob!"

"You're *in love* with me…"

"I'm *in love* with you, Jacob White!"

I thrust deep inside her. She screamed and I withdrew. I swear to God, as punked out as it seemed, tears were rolling down my cheeks. Damn me!

"Yes!" she moaned. I slid deep inside her again. The tension mounted as we rocked against each other.

"I love you! I love you! I love you!" she sang and moaned with every thrust of our bodies.

Mine burned like fire at her words, and I pressed forward.

I could tell by her breathing that she was about to come. I could tell by the way she gripped me inside her, squeezing me involuntarily.

"Oh, damn!" I cried out. I was losing the battle. Goddamn, I was losing it! And I was coming, tingling, convulsing along with my lady.

At that moment nothing mattered. No disagreements had ever taken place. No words of pain and hurt had ever passed between us. Nothing mattered but this feeling.

Absolutely nothing.

CHAPTER 11

Kimberla

No bad dreams haunted me last night. No bogeyman tormented me. I woke up with a smile on my face. It was a sweet change for me. I felt so good, so rested and at peace. I glanced over at the source of my happiness. He was gone. I frowned, got up, and walked to the bathroom, where I could hear him speaking to someone.

"What did Kyte say?" I heard him ask. "Well, just wait 'til he talks to Kimberla first. Yes, I know you want the case, Lo-Lo, but if you call Kimberla before Kyte can break the news to her, let's just say it wouldn't be good."

I gasped, alerting him to my presence. He was sitting on the edge of the tub, looking up at me with a surprised guilty look on his face.

All my peace and happiness vanished. Here this man was, sitting in my house, having just spent the night making love to me, talking to another woman!

We stared at each other for what felt like several long dragging minutes. I finally took a deep breath and tried to compose myself.

"What was that about?" I asked. My voice was so quiet I could barely hear myself.

"I—I... That was Lolita."

"Oh, I know who she is. It's cute how you call her Lo-Lo. Pet name, huh? But my question is, why are you calling her in my house? And what is this about her wanting a case and not telling me about it?"

I would have laughed at the pathetically caught look on Jacob's face if I wasn't so damn angry. And his hesitancy wasn't easing my anger one damn bit.

"Answer me, Jacob!"

"Kimberla, you know she's with our division now—"

"I don't know anything! All I know is she's the same bitch that was at your house in the middle of the night two weeks ago. The same bitch you used to be involved with. And you got the nerve to call her while you're here with me?"

"Don't talk ugly like that, baby. That's not you."

Oh no, this Negro was not trying to patronize me.

"What?" I almost screamed. "Don't tell me how to talk, Jacob!"

He shook his head from side to side and then took a deep breath. His hands were gesturing all over the place as if he didn't know what to do with them. He was upset. Frankly I didn't care how he felt. I wanted answers.

"There is nothing between Lolita and me. I've told you that before. We are just friends, honestly."

"Yeah, right. And what was this about her wanting the case? What case, Jacob?"

Silence followed.

"Well?"

"Look," he said, sighing heavily. "You need to talk to Kyte about this."

"Talk to Kyte? Were you and her talking about the case Micah and I were working on, Jacob? Have you been working against me to have Kyte give my case to Lolita?"

My words came out almost as if I were strangling. I felt so hurt, so betrayed. I was choking inside.

"Of course not," Jacob lamented. "But you can't work alone, Kimberla. Lolita is a damn good agent. I say talk to Kyte because he would be the best one to explain this to you. Especially now with you being so worked up and upset. You aren't listening to a word I'm saying!"

I gave Jacob a quick look-over. For the first time I noticed that he was already dressed. I supposed he didn't have plans to spend the day. At this point that was fine by me. I walked out of the bathroom, into my bedroom, and picked his keys up off the end table. I handed them to him.

"You have no right to get in my business just so you can support your other woman's career."

"What? Ugh, girl!"

He slammed his fist against my bedroom wall, causing one of my African art portraits to fall. It hit the floor with a crash.

"That will cost one fifty, please," I said sarcastically.

"Fuck that picture!"

"Don't curse at me…"

I'd had enough. My head was throbbing and I was feeling sick to my stomach. I leaned against the wall and covered my face with my hands. After gathering my composure, I looked at Jacob solemnly.

"You know, Jacob. I really don't need this. I don't trust you. And without trust we have nothing. I feel betrayed." I gestured toward him. "And since you are obviously already dressed and ready, I suggest you leave."

"You suggest I leave? You know what? I am going to leave. I'm so tired of your insecurity, and I'm sick to death of the games, Kimberla."

He walked out of my bedroom and to the living room door. My heart was racing but I followed him.

"I haven't done anything wrong," he said, opening the front door. "Lolita called me, not the other way around."

"So, I guess she calls you a lot, huh? If you can't see how disgusting and fishy this looks, it's because you don't want to see it."

Jacob paused for a moment. "Forget it," he said under his breath. He took a step out the door, then stopped. My heart stopped also.

I didn't want him to go. I wished somehow he would stay. I felt so confused!

"By the way, I almost forgot." He pulled some cash out of his wallet and stuffed it in my hands. "I don't want you to say I owe you anything. Good-bye, Kimmy," he said sadly.

* * *

Two hours later I was waiting in Kyte Williams's office. It irritated me whenever I had to wait for someone. But then again I hadn't come to headquarters feeling very cheery in the first place.

The room embodied the spirit and personality of Captain Kyte Williams, from the dark decor, black shades, black leather couch, which I sat on, black marble desktop and matching leather recliner, to the numerous awards and medals of honor on the wall. This was definitely Kyte's domain.

I hadn't bothered to call him before dressing and leaving my condo in a rush. But surprise, surprise, he had called me while I was en route to headquarters, asking me to meet him. His call fueled my suspicions that Jacob hadn't wasted any time filling his Lo-Lo in on our morning confrontation. She, thereafter, must have called Kyte.

A male's betrayal should never surprise me. With Jacob, I still couldn't quite stomach the shock.

What made things worse was that he had managed to seduce out of me the fact that I was in love with him. But love or no love, I didn't trust him. I couldn't trust any man. And his actions validated my reasons. He knew I wouldn't want to work with his ex-lover. Was I being unreasonable? That's relative to opinion. Unprofessional? Maybe. But the whole situation was very personal for me, so my feelings on the matter, as far as I was concerned, really didn't have to be professional.

The door opened suddenly and in walked Kyte. He was all smiles.

"Kimberla!"

"Took you long enough," I said wryly.

Kyte laughed. "Didn't know you missed me so much."

I didn't smile back.

"Hmm...okay, Kimberla, what's wrong?"

I stood up and faced him. "You know what's wrong, Kyte, and you know why I'm here. Are you taking my case away after you promised me you wouldn't?"

Kyte gave a deep sigh. "Oh, Kimberla, what am I gonna do with you?" He walked over to his desk and flopped down casually in his leather recliner.

"I just want to know what's going on," I explained. "I know you think I'm too emotionally involved—"

"Do *you* think you're too emotionally involved?" he cut in. "Listen, you and Latimer had gotten really close, so I know it's not just about solving the Soroco case and all these other murders for you anymore."

I closed my eyes and took a deep breath.

"Please, are you taking the case away from me or not?" I asked.

Kyte leaned back in his recliner and stared at me, as if measuring me up. "I want to see where your mind is right now, Kimberla."

"What do you mean where my mind is? My mind is on my job. I am feeling much better and I want to finish what Micah and I started. I don't feel I should be penalized for getting attacked. That comes along with the job. I'm still a very capable agent, Kyte. A knock on my head didn't kill all my senses."

"It's not about your capabilities. It's about protecting you, Kimberla. It's about your mentality in this case." He reached out and took my hand in his. "Look, for the record, I plan to give you a chance to continue with the case."

I breathed a sigh of relief. "Thank you, Kyte. I promise I'll be okay, and—"

"I've assigned you a new partner," he cut in. "I'm not sure if you've met her before. But you may have heard of her."

Oh Lawd, I thought. I knew he was going to say…

"Her name is Lolita Mason. She just transferred here from one of our West Coast divisions."

"Yes, I've heard of her," I croaked.

"Good!" Kyte smiled. "I believe she and Jacob worked together a few times when he was in Los Angeles."

They did more than work together, I mused inwardly. I fought hard to keep my facial expression bland and unreadable.

Kyte continued, looking pretty satisfied. "Anyhow, I figured you two have similar working styles and would complement each other perfectly. As a matter of fact, she's waiting outside my office. Hold up a moment."

He put his hand to his intercom buzzer. "Send Lolita in," he told his secretary.

Kyte looked at me and grinned. I gave him a cheesy, tight smile in return, but inside, I wanted to throw up.

CHAPTER 12

Frederick, Maryland

Steven Michaels worked what was typically called the graveyard shift. He was a night manager for a local Wal-Mart Supercenter, and he loved it. The hard, physical labor didn't bother him at all. It wasn't that he had an early death wish or a feenin' for indentured servitude, and as hard as he worked, sometimes one would think he did. But he simply loved the fact that working nights freed him during the daytime. Daytime was his most productive time. He loved that his wife of ten years wasn't home on his off time. She was an RN at a nursing home, a full hour away.

This gave him what he craved, the freedom to hunt. Steven didn't hunt animals; not the four-legged ones at least. He preferred the hunting of pleasure, human pleasure. He preferred the most debased, carnal pleasures. For Steven, that was something his wife couldn't supply him in most cases, and in other cases, wouldn't. Simply put, it was anal lovin'. He didn't care where that pleasure came from, whether it was man, woman, or beast.

He walked into his two-story family home, which he

shared with his wife and nine-year-old son. He dropped his keys and jacket and rushed to his favorite place, the family room, and then logged on to his computer. The family dog, Flannel, ran over to greet him, barking in delight.

"What's up, boy!" Steven said, patting Flannel's head playfully. He didn't want to give Flannel too much of his time. He preferred to give the Internet his time and attention, especially the Ebony-Bi chat room.

With his user name, Sexcrimez01, he was a regular visitor in the chat. This morning, however, he was in for a disappointment. It was empty.

"Damn!" Steven exclaimed.

Even if he couldn't arrange, as he normally did, to meet someone for a discreet sex hookup, he'd hoped to at least find someone for some hot phone sex, or cyber. He'd just have to get his own rocks off, he thought.

Just as he was clicking out of the chat room, he received an Instant Message. The user name was a female he had talked to once before, and whom he had met in the chat room. Catwomyn75.

Catwomyn75: Hello.

Sexcrimez01: What's going on?

Catwomyn75: I'm bored and horny.

Sexcrimez01: Oh, really?

Steven's sex began to rise. He had been thinking about some man-on-man loving earlier, but he was never one to discriminate.

Sexcrimez01: You never did tell me what part of Maryland you're from.

Catwomyn75: Y? Are you going to CUM take care of this 4 me?

Sexcrimez01: Depends on how far I have to CUM. LOL.

This woman intrigued Steven. Her wit, her open and honest sexuality, made him want her. As far as he was concerned, there weren't too many women who wanted the goods and weren't too afraid to ask for it. Those were the types that made him turn to getting his rocks off with the brothas. His prude-ass wife had a lot to do with it, too. Steven didn't feel he was gay. He was just a freak! He didn't understand how his wife could expect him to be married to her for ten years, buy the house and a car, give her a kid, yet the bitch wouldn't even give him head.

Sexcrimez01: Baby, tell me where you at. Let's do something about this horniness. :)

Catwomyn75: LOL@the smiley face. How about you tell me where you are? Or better yet, let's meet somewhere neutral. I'm just a lone woman; can't trust just anybody, you know. Too many crazies out here.

Sexcrimez01: Yeah, I feel ya. But I gotz to be careful, too. How do I know you aren't some sexy diva wanting to chop a brotha up and shit? LOL.

Catwomyn75: Well, you really don't know that, now, do you? LOL.

Steven was typing with one hand and keeping himself stimulated with the other. His body was getting hotter by the minute.

Sexcrimez01: Damn, you got me hard. What you into?

Catwomyn75: Why don't we stop chatting and start doing.

Sexcrimez01: I'll come to you.

Catwomyn75: No. I'll come to you. You said you were in Frederick, right? How about I meet you at a hotel? There's one right before the Frederick Scott Key Mall.

Sexcrimez01: What time?

Steven's heart was beating faster and faster.

Catwomyn75: It's 8:30 now. I can be there by 9:30.

Sexcrimez01: Cool! Bring something sexy to wear. Something easy for me to take off.

Catwomyn75: LOL. Remember, don't be late.

An hour was too late for Steven. But he had to follow

her lead. That's the problem with ladies: they had the power when it came to sex. Catwomyn was a bit weird, he thought. But whatever she had in store for him, he would be her willful playmate.

After a quick shower and personal prep job, Steven was making his way down I-64 to the hotel. It was a quick drive, or maybe he just drove a little too fast. The car his soon-to-be playmate described, a dark-blue Jeep Liberty, was waiting at the entry doors, just as she said it would be. He honked at her and then drove to the guest parking lot. She followed.

She pulled up beside Steven and smiled. He mused inside when he realized he didn't even know her name. He pulled down the window.

"What's your name, babe?" he asked her.

"Jami," she replied. "Why don't you go in and get the room, and I'll wait for you out here?"

Steven nodded in agreement. He wasn't gonna argue with the lady. He wanted to get in her pants too badly to do that.

They shared a cold Pepsi that Jami had gotten out of the machine on her way up to the room. She was taking too long to get settled, as far as Steven was concerned. He looked at his watch. He wanted to hurry up, take care of his business with her, and get home so he could get a few hours of sleep before his son came home from school. Steven watched as she took another swallow of her soda.

"Why don't you put that down and show me how good you can swallow something else?" he whispered.

Jami looked at him and smiled. "You don't mince words, do you?"

"I have no reason to, when I know what I want," he responded.

He reached over and ran his fingers over the imprint of her breast swell. She was one fine-looking woman. He pinched her nipple through the fabric.

"Wait a minute," she said, pulling back slightly.

"What's to wait for? This is why we are here. Come on, lady, I'm not here to play schoolgirl games."

He pushed her back down to the bed, and then pulled her hair up so he could get to her neck. Jami reached up, as if to stop him. She gasped when Steven grabbed her wrist, causing the thin charm bracelet she wore to break loose and fall to the floor.

Damn the bracelet. He almost laughed at the look of shock on her face. But damn if he was gonna allow her to waste the good money he spent for this hotel, watching her drink a Pepsi. He knocked it out of her hand and had her beneath him, seconds later, grinding against her. He could feel her struggling. He liked that. She was breathing hard.

"Okay—okay," she said. Steven looked down at her wet, full lips. She gave him a crooked smile. "You're an aggressive man, aren't you?" she whispered.

"You like it rough?" he asked.

"Sometimes. You just caught me by surprise."

"Mmm…" Steven moaned, reaching down beneath her skirt. He cupped her sex, and then moved his head down to her breasts, biting her nipples again, then to her stomach, lifting her skirt at the same time.

"Please, wait," she said.

He was having none of that. He moved down lower, till his mouth was covering her sex. He started sucking and licking her through the silky fabric.

"Ohhhhh," she moaned. She thrust her hips up in an arched fashion. Steven pushed her panties aside, and planted his lips against her thick, musty ones. He sucked them into his mouth, along with her clit, flicking and swirling the fat nub as if it were an M&M candy.

"No! Yes! No! Oh, yesss!" Jami moaned and screamed at the same time.

Her body wasn't as confused, it seemed, as her mind. With each no, she held Steven's head tighter against her. He was digging his tongue deep inside her now, slurping at her inner tunnel, then moving back to nibble on her aching clit.

This woman acted as if she hadn't had her cat eaten in ages, Steven thought, almost laughing aloud. She was bouncing so hard the bed was banging against the wall. He thrust his fingers deeper inside her, setting off an avalanche of sparks. Jami's body was shaking, her orgasms hard and long against his mouth.

Steven lay there, kissing her inner thighs for a moment and smiling. Damn, he was good, he thought. He had looked up at her to voice his thoughts out loud when he noticed her holding a needle in her hand.

"What's that for?" he asked.

Alarms suddenly went off in his head, and he jumped. Her hand seemed to move at the same time, and Steven felt a sharp sting on the side of his neck.

"Ouch! You fuckin' bitch!" he shouted. He slapped the needle from her hand, and was thinking of slapping the life out of her, until he felt a numbing in his body. He looked at her eyes. "What—what did you do?"

She pushed him off her. And then like the Angel of Death, Jami kissed Steven Michaels good-bye.

CHAPTER 13

Kimberla

This was going to be harder than I had imagined. I had to swallow my personal feelings and act like it was all business, dealing with Lolita. Things had gone smooth during the meeting with Kyte. I smiled and pretended I liked the ho, never letting it be known that I wanted to wrap my hands around her trifling neck and let her be the next murder victim. I guess I felt kind of bad with my unholy thoughts. But I don't know too many women who wouldn't feel the same way I did.

That was yesterday. Today I was sitting in my car, waiting for her to come out of the bathroom at the restaurant we had just had lunch at. Neither of us seemed to want to talk about Jacob. We focused on the case and matters related to it. Like whether the person who committed these murders could possibly have anything to do with who killed Micah, and tried to knock my head off. I had decided I was gonna let go of the insecure feelings that were causing me to lose self-respect and my own dignity. From reading up on Lolita's files, I knew there was no reason for me not to know she would make a great partner, once I was able to squash the personal. It would just take more effort on my part.

A couple of minutes later Lolita made her appearance. I tried to give her a smile as she got in the car, but I was sure it came off as tight and insincere.

"Sorry I took so long," she lamented.

"It's cool."

We rode in silence. My favorite Fantasia song, "Free Yourself," was playing on the radio. I couldn't help but wish I could free myself from this irritating, uncomfortable situation.

"What's the fastest route to your place?" I asked her.

"Kimmy—"

"It's Kimberla. Only my family and closest friends call me Kimmy."

A look of embarrassment washed over Lolita's face. "Okay, sorry. Listen," she said with a sigh. "This is not gonna work. How can we work together if there is so much tension between us? I know you don't like me because of Jacob, but there is no way we are going to do a good job in this case if we are hardly talking."

There was silence after Lolita's rant. Mainly because I had to breathe inwardly so I wouldn't flip and go off on her ass. I had made a promise to myself that I'd keep my interaction with her professional if it killed me, but she was surely making that difficult by bringing up Jacob.

"Lolita, we've been talking about the Soroco case all

day, so I really don't know what you mean. Secondly, I beg your pardon about Jacob. He and I are not together and I couldn't care less how he feels about you. The only way we are going to have a problem is if you bring him up to me again. Our dealings need only to be working together to figure out who's doing these killings. Now if you feel you can't work with me, if you feel you can't handle it, we can just let Kyte know so he can put someone else on the case."

Lolita looked shocked. I myself felt rather proud of my classy response. Especially knowing what type of temper I sometimes had.

"Wow…" she whispered.

"Yeah. Wow," I repeated. "Now do you want to tell me a quicker way to get you home?" I gave Lolita a sweet, innocent smile.

Just as I asked that, my cell phone rang. I picked it up, feeling relieved at the interruption.

"Hello?"

"Kimberla, is Lolita with you?" It was Kyte.

"Yes, she is."

"Great. Put your phone on speaker. I need to talk to the both of you."

I pushed the tiny speaker phone button on my cell before he finished his request. I gave a shoulder shrug at Lolita's curious expression.

"Go ahead," I told Kyte.

"Okay, you both, listen. There was a body found a

couple of hours ago in Frederick. Same MO as the others. I need you to get up there ASAP."

I glanced at Lolita. Our expressions read the same. This thing was getting more and more serious, and this murderer had to be stopped.

Jacob

I watched my daughter position her Barbies in the huge, pink dollhouse that I had gotten her for Christmas. The sunlight bounced off her light-brown face, but it didn't need to. I could always see the sunlight in my baby's face even on a cloudy day.

The past couple of days since I had last seen Kimberla had indeed been cloudy for me. But Bree made it better. I decided to stop sitting around feeling gloomy and take care of the most important person in my life: my daughter.

"Daddy, when are you gonna fix lunch?" she asked me.

I laughed.

"You're hungry already? We just had breakfast less than two hours ago!"

"Yes, but you fixed it late."

"You wouldn't get your butt out of the bed is why," I said with a grin.

Bree ran, suddenly making a tackle for my lap that would put an NFL linebacker to shame. We both fell over in a heap.

"Whoa!" I exclaimed. I gave her a big hug. "You're strong as an ox, girl."

Bree gave me a mischievous smile. "Well, you said I get it from my mama."

"Yeah, you do," I said softly. "And you look just like her, strong and beautiful."

It amazed me how much she really did look like her mother, and had her beautiful spirit. There wasn't a day that passed that I didn't pray I was doing things right. It was hard working so much and trying to raise a child at the same time.

I sighed inwardly. I had hoped that Kimberla, who actually loved Bree, would be my partner in helping me finish what my late wife and I had started.

"When is Miss Kimberla coming to get me again?" Bree asked, as if reading my mind.

I took a deep breath at that one. I knew that Kimmy loved Bree, but I wasn't so sure how she would deal with things, now that her and my relationship was over.

"I'll call her later and you can talk to her, okay?"

"Okay," Bree said, sighing slightly. She jumped out of my lap and flopped down beside me. "Why hasn't she been over to get me? I miss her, Daddy."

I stared into the dark brown eyes that looked like her mother's. This was one dilemma I hadn't counted on. I didn't know how to explain to Bree that Kimberla and I weren't seeing each other anymore. For sure she was too young to understand.

"Let's find something for lunch, okay?"

Before Bree could respond, the phone rang. I rushed to grab it. It was Anthony, a private investigator I had hired to dig deeper into the disappearance of Malcolm Johnson. Even though the bureau had closed the case and officially decided he was dead, I wasn't so convinced. Especially after my drunk visions the other week.

"Jacob, whassup, buddy?"

"Hold up a second. Let me move to the bedroom," I said in a low voice. I looked down at Bree, who at this point was pulling on the leg of my pants. "Give me a few minutes, okay, baby?"

"But, Daddy!"

I didn't mean to ignore her, but I was already heading to the bedroom.

"All right, Anthony, what did you find out?"

He cleared his throat. "Okay, get this. That dude that Kimberla took out? He used to work for Johnson's sister. Bailey Hamilton. Bailey is married to some rich senator up in Boston."

"Hmm...so there is a connection. You think she has something to do with Micah and Kimberla's attack?"

"I'm not sure," Anthony said. "You want me to go to Boston and talk to her?"

"You took the words right out of my mouth. As a matter of fact, I'm going with you."

Kimberla

The scene was one you would never imagine seeing in a small, mountainous place like Frederick. It looked almost normal, until you got to the bed. There, obviously, some type of struggle had taken place. The victim was a black male, looked to be in his thirties, and lying on his side with his eyes wide open. As with the other cases, FBI agents along with local Frederick police officers crowded around, taking pictures and looking for clues.

"What's his name?" I asked the investigator in charge.

"Steven Michaels," he said, looking at his notepad. "Don't know who would want to kill this guy. According to the hotel records, he was just a manager for the local Wal-Mart."

"That's a big man to kill," Lolita noted. She put on her gloves and started feeling around.

"Big man or not, somebody did it. And by the looks of things, I'm still thinking it's a woman," I said.

Lolita looked at me oddly. "Why is that?"

I walked over to the body, and pointed to different parts of his body.

"For one thing, even though we can tell there was some sort of a struggle, by looking at the bed area, that is, that struggle didn't include a physical fight. It was the same with all the other victims. Soroco wasn't found in a hotel room, but that's the only difference. A man would fight, if it were another man."

I pointed to a bloodied needle mark on the victim's neck. "I got a feeling this guy saw it coming, so he had time to at least jump. The other victims did not."

"So you think it was a sexual struggle?"

"Sexual enough for him to take his clothes off," I said with a laugh.

Lolita bent down and picked up a small charm of a cat. "Well, this is interesting," she said.

"Hmm...yes, it is," I agreed. "I think we need to go talk to his wife."

CHAPTER 14

Catwomyn75

She let the hot water of her shower dance over her. Inside she was shaking. Self-disgust made her feel dirty, trashy; she wanted to throw up. She scrubbed hard, hoping to wash away the memory of what she had allowed to happen. She didn't need men. She hated them, all of them!

She scrubbed harder, oblivious to the raw spots on her skin she irritated more and more with the soapstone. Blood began to seep slowly from her tender pores, blending with the warm ribbons of water. She didn't feel a thing. Her eyes were closed as tears ran down her face.

She remembered when she first saw them. The pain was fresh as if it were just yesterday. Her mind and heart took her back. The pain sizzled within her being, yet she tried to snuff it out by scrubbing even harder. It didn't work.

Years of happiness can turn into an eternity of pain in one twinkling of the eye.

She'd had a long day at work, but as always had come home to fix her man a delicious dinner. This time it consisted of fried chicken, sweet potatoes, and buttered cabbage. Complete with some red Kool-Aid. Aiming to please was always her way when it came to her husband. Some successful women felt they had to flex their strength and success, and let their men know they were so-called equals. She didn't feel that way. He pampered her in all the ways she needed, and in return, she treated him like her king.

Her husband wasn't home yet. So after getting dinner started, she decided to surprise him with an e-mail. (He was still at the office.) She started to make her way up the stairs to her computer, but then noticed he had left his laptop bag in the hallway. It would be easier to just use his computer and watch dinner at the same time. She grabbed the bag, took his computer out, and booted it up. Just as the Windows logo was coming on, the telephone rang. She jumped up to get it.

"Hello?" she said.

"Babe, it's me. I wanted to let you know I'll be working late tonight with Gary, so I'll just grab something to eat here, okay?"

Talk about disappointed! "What? I already started cooking! I'm fixing your favorites."

"Aw, babe. I'll just take some of it to work with me tomorrow. I gotta go. I love you!"

"Damnit!" she exclaimed, feeling disappointment wash over her.

After thinking about it for a second, she decided she would just finish cooking and take him a plate. She hated warmed-up food.

An hour later dinner was done, and she was piling a plateful to take over to him. It suddenly hit her that she had completely forgotten to send the "I love you" e-mail. The laptop was already booted up and connected to their home network, but she was surprised when she opened the face of it to see an instant message on the screen.

Sxx24: I wanna taste you.

What did that mean? Who would send that to her husband? Some online freak lady, she thought.

"Hmph!" she said out loud to herself. She closed the laptop, grabbed the hot plate of food she had just fixed, and walked out the door.

It took less than ten minutes for her to reach his office. The parking lot was dark, and almost empty, but for a few cars. She quickly made her way inside, deciding to take the stairs rather than the elevator. When she got to her husband's office, she paused for a moment as she heard the unmistakable muffled sounds of moaning. She opened the door. At first she didn't see anyone but her husband, standing in front of his desk. His hips were moving back and forth; his head was thrown back and his mouth was open, lips trembling. She gasped when she looked down farther, and saw who was beneath her husband. Squealing like a prostitute was his so-called friend and partner, Gary Flowers.

Her gasp alerted them. When her husband turned around and saw her, his eyes widened. He opened his mouth to say her name, but she was already heading for the elevator, in shock.

She was rocking back and forth in the recliner when he came in the door. She was silent; no tears, just silence. Her husband came inside the bedroom and sat on the bed.

"I'm sorry. I never meant for you to find out this way," he said quietly.

"So you're gay?"

"I don't know what I am," he whispered with a sigh. "All I know is I can't live this—this fake existence anymore. I haven't been happy for a long time."

Oddly enough, she wasn't even angry. She felt numb, dead.

"Sleep on the couch," she finally said. "I don't want you anywhere near me."

He sighed again and went to the closet to grab a blanket. He didn't see her coming up behind him with the sharp hypodermic needle in her hand. Just as he was about to turn away from the closet, she stabbed him in the back of the neck. He jumped, but the medicine worked fast, as she knew it would. He fell face-forward into the closet. She grabbed him before he hit the floor. She didn't want him to have any bruises, thus leaving it suspect that his death was anything but a surprise heart attack. She pulled him to the bed, leaning over him, and kissing him softly on the lips. This time, the tears flowed freely.

* * *

Catwomyn75 was born that night, and she had been struggling to kill the pain, brought by betrayal, over and over again, ever since.

The water had long gone cold, yet still she stood there, shivering and crying. No matter how many she killed, no matter the excuses she gave herself—that she was doing all women a favor by wiping bisexual liars off the face of the earth—deep inside she was doing it for herself. She was trying to find a remedy for a pain that had started the night she found out that her beloved husband, the man she had vowed her life to, was sleeping with a man.

How many times can you kill a man before the pain stops? The answer never came. No man was safe, and she would never have a moment's peace, until it did.

Kimberla

Sunlight lit up the cozy townhome. It gave a fake feeling of warmth, but it was pretty obvious that sadness and chill filled the hearts of the family of Steven Michaels.

I felt really terrible. Steven Michaels's wife had the typical look of devastation on her face as we questioned her. But mostly I felt horrible for his son. He sat beside his mother, not a tear in his eyes, trying to be strong. But his little body was trembling. This was the worst part of dealing with homicides: the family left behind, and trying to explain the unexplainable of why.

"Mrs. Michaels, I know this is hard for you," Lolita said. "We really need to know if there is anything you can tell us about your husband, or anyone you think could have wanted to harm him."

I gave Lolita a hard look. Why she would ask Mrs. Michaels that question around her son was beyond my comprehension.

As if reading my mind, Mrs. Michaels looked at her son and said, "Honey, go next door and keep Ms. Thomas company for a little while, okay?"

"Mama, I wanna stay with you!" he cried.

Mrs. Michaels pulled him close to her in a tight hug. "I really need you to listen to me, sweetie. I need to talk to the policewomen for a little while, in private."

The dejected little boy relented, reluctantly. Again, feelings of pity washed over me. After he had left, Lolita and I turned our attention to Mrs. Michaels.

"I don't know who could have wanted him dead," she said. "My husband had a lot of secrets."

"Secrets?" I asked.

"What kind of secrets?" Lolita probed.

She was getting on my damn nerves. I was the head agent in this case, and if she was as experienced as everyone tried to make her out to be, she should have re-membered that while questioning family or witnesses, the agent in charge is the one who asks the questions. I would remind her of that later.

"My husband was a cheater. He thought I didn't know about it, but I did."

That wasn't much of a shock, but it was a shock that Mrs. Michaels seemed to know about it, and was so calm in her statement.

"How do you know he cheated?" I asked.

She stood up and walked toward the family room. We followed her. Once there, she sat down at the computer desk and signed on to the Internet.

"This is his user name?" asked Lolita.

The name read Sexcrimez01. That name was an understatement considering what had happened to him.

"Yes. He deletes his e-mails. He may have suspected that I knew about his indiscretions." Mrs. Michaels's face was blanched. "Or he just may have been covering his tracks."

"If you knew he was cheating, why did you never confront him?" I asked her.

She laughed without humor. "And say what? Agent Bacon, I have a son to take care of. I had a life I cherished. To be honest, I wasn't about to rock my boat over this. As long as he was discreet and didn't bring it home, I dealt with it. Isn't that what women are supposed to do?"

The fact she felt that way was pretty sad, I thought. The fact that any woman felt she had to stay with a cheater was a sad testimony to relationships, period. I couldn't help but think about Jacob and my situation. I looked at Lolita quietly. She looked back and shook her head.

"Do you mind if I take a look?" she asked Mrs. Michaels, nodding toward the computer.

"No, but you won't find anything. Like I said, he normally deleted any e-mails."

Lolita clicked on the Mail window, then on Managed E-mail, and then Saved. I was very curious as to what she was doing. To all of our surprise, a long list of e-mails popped up. Lolita looked rather proud of herself.

"See the thing about some internet providers are that, even if you delete e-mails they are automatically saved on the server. We should be able to find any woman he has been talking to and at least get a lead to something."

"Women? I'm not talking about women," said Mrs. Michaels.

"But you said you felt he was cheating," I said in confusion.

"Oh, he was. For the past year, I know for a fact that my husband was cheating. But not just with women. Actually the women were the least of my worries. If needed, I could compete with them."

She walked over to a window and opened the blinds. She took a deep breath and then covered her face with her hands as if she were trying to compose herself. Finally she looked back over at Lolita and me.

"My husband was bisexual."

CHAPTER 15

Jacob

The BWI Airport was crowded for midweek flying. I figured this was due to the Labor Day weekend. Anthony and I had already turned in our tickets and were waiting the twenty minutes we had left for our flight to be called. I figured I should call and talk to Kimberla about Bree before we got on our plane. She and I hadn't been talking very much, and I didn't want her to know where I was headed, but the disappointment in my baby's voice yesterday was on my mind. Not to mention, I missed Kimberla. I missed hearing from her, touching her. I even missed arguing with her.

Anthony tapped me on the arm, getting my attention.

"So what are we gonna do first when we get to Boston?" he asked.

I stuck a piece of Bubblicious bubblegum in my mouth, chewing it quietly. "Well, no use wasting time. I want to see Bailey Hamilton's reaction when we ask her about her brother."

"You really believe this guy is still alive, don't you?"

"I don't know, Anthony. I mean, like I told you before,

I was drunk the night Kimberla and Micah were attacked. I guess sometimes we can hallucinate. But I can't get the vision out of my head. And I can't take any chances with Kimberla."

"Whoa." Anthony whistled. "Brotha, you are in love!"

"Shut the fuck up."

"No, for real." He laughed. "Ain't nuttin' wrong with that. I think it's a boo-ti-ful thang!"

His so-called analysis of my feelings irritated me, although he was right. I didn't need anyone trying to figure me out.

"I need to make a call real quick," I told him. "I'll be right back."

He nodded, laughing as he stuck his head into a *Sports Illustrated* magazine. I walked over to the coffee café, sat down, and dialed her number.

"Hello?" she said, startling me at first because she had answered on the first ring.

"Oh—Kimberla, how you doing?"

"I'm fine."

Her quietness let me know she still had an attitude with me. That bothered me.

"Listen, Bree has been asking when you're gonna come get her. I know you and I have our problems, but they don't include her, do they?"

"Jacob, how could you even ask me that? You know I love Bree. And no, our problems have nothing to do with her." She sighed a little. "What did she say? You tell her we've broken up?"

I closed my eyes, wanting to reach out and touch her through the telephone. I opened them again when I heard the ten-minute warning for my flight.

"Jacob, where are you? Sounds like you're at an airport."

"I am. I have to leave for a few days to check on something," I said evasively. "And no, I haven't told her about us. I think she's too young to really understand that. I was hoping you would get her, spend a little time with her, though."

"Yes, I will… Jacob, I know it's not my business anymore, but where exactly are you going?"

I chose to ignore that question. Kimberla was the type of person that never allowed one to evade answering anything. So I took advantage of my situation and said, "Miss Carter is staying with her at my place. Call her, okay? I gotta go. My flight has already been called once."

"Jacob?"

"I still love you, Kimmy. Call Bree when you get a chance. I'll talk to you soon."

Kimberla

No, he didn't hang up in my face! I absolutely hated that. I hated even more that I missed Jacob as much as I did. After he hung up, I sat for a moment, thinking about his last words. He still loved me, he said. I didn't want to focus on his words. I needed to focus on my work. But that was so hard, especially working with Lolita. My mind stayed occupied with Jacob, and his call gave me a guilt complex about Bree. I hadn't meant to ignore her. She didn't deserve to suffer due to her dad's and my relationship issues. That was one of the problems when dealing with a man who had children. You committed yourself, not only to him, but to them. Bree had connected emotionally with me, ever since Jacob and I had started seriously dating. I guess it was never a big concern of mine, since I never thought we would end up like this.

I stood at the bathroom mirror and soaped my face with Noxzema. I figured I would relax a bit and call Bree before she went to bed. My day had been long and emotionally taxing, and I wanted to get an early night.

It was kind of hard for me to admit, but Lolita wasn't so bad, at least professionally she wasn't. For the first time since these murders had started, there were some real leads. Mrs. Michaels's revelation about her husband's computer habits had given us new options and possible ways to connect the three murder victims; outside of the way they had been killed, of course. Lolita's computer literacy would help in finding out more. Her idea was to confiscate the computers of all the victims, and see if there were any e-mails or pictures that would coincide with Steven Michaels's.

I was showered and chilling out on my silk Japanese covers. I picked up the telephone to dial Bree, but jumped when the phone rang while in my hand. I laughed at my nerves.

"You're getting old, girl," I said to myself. "Hello?"

"I missed the first time," a voice said, "but I never miss twice."

"Excuse me? Who is this?"

The voice on the phone was muffled, and obviously someone who was trying to disguise himself.

"Just know this, I always pay my debts. I owe you, bitch." He hung up the phone.

An icy feeling of dread came over me. Not because I was afraid of what that lunatic had to say. I wasn't really afraid of anyone. What bothered me the most was that I did not know who I was dealing with. Somehow I had a feeling it had something to do with my attack, and with Micah's murder.

My intercom buzzed, alerting me that someone was at the door. Not taking any chances, I wrapped my housecoat, snug around me, grabbed my pistol, and walked to the door.

"Who is it?" I said, speaking loudly at the voice box.

"Joan Latimer. I really need to talk to you, please."

Oh my God! I thought. It was Micah's mother. I tucked the pistol in the pocket of my housecoat and quickly opened the door.

"I'm sorry," I said right away, feeling really guilty for coming to the door with a weapon, even though she didn't know that. "I wasn't expecting anyone."

"No," she said, "I'm the one that should apologize. It is rather late and I would have called, but I didn't know your number."

We stood there looking at each other awkwardly for a

moment. It was pretty easy to see where Micah had gotten his dark good looks. His mother was a smaller, feminine version of him. However, her face didn't have the happy-go-lucky look that Micah had always worn. Her look was one of pain and suffering, a look only a mother who had lost her only child could wear.

"I really am sorry about Micah, Ms. Latimer," I whispered.

She looked at me, and tears filled her eyes. They almost beckoned my own to fall.

"I just don't understand," she said. "Why did this happen? Why did it happen to Micah?"

I grabbed her hands in mine. "I promise you, we are doing everything possible to find those responsible."

"I thought the man you shot that night was responsible?"

"Oh, he was. But there have to be more involved. We don't think he even knew Micah, or me. There is a bigger picture and we need to examine it more carefully."

"Yeah, right." She yanked her hands back, almost angrily. "Doesn't really matter, nothing can bring my son back to me, will it? Oh!" she exclaimed, covering her face. "I don't even know why I'm here. I—I don't know what I'm looking for."

"I'm so sorry…"

"It's not your fault." She shook her head sadly. "It's just been so hard to accept that I'll never see him again. Micah was all I had. Was he happy? His last hours, he was happy, wasn't he?"

"Ms. Latimer, Micah was honestly one of the happiest people I knew. He always had a way of making everyone around him feel like our problems weren't as bad as we make them all to be. Like he said, there is always someone worse off. He was a wonderful person."

Micah's mother took a deep breath of relief. I really wished I could find my own peace so easily.

I reached out to take her into my arms in mutual mourning. It would be a long time before I would be able to forgive myself for being able to save me, and not Micah.

Ms. Latimer hugged me back at that moment. I could almost hear Micah saying, "See, Kimmy, it ain't so bad after all."

I almost believed those words.

CHAPTER 16

Jacob

Due to our last-minute flight reservations, we ended up with an overnight layover; thus, we slept in the freakin' airport. By the time we landed at Logan International in Boston, both Anthony and I were extremely burnt out. After renting a Grand Cherokee, we ended up at the Holiday Inn. For sure it wasn't a five-star spot, but it would suffice.

"Whoa!" Anthony exclaimed. "This room smells like a mix of old piss and cigarettes."

"Okay, Forrest Gump." I gave him a wry smile.

"I'm serious, man. We asked for a smoke-free joint. I don't even wanna be able to smell that shit."

"Well, I tell you what." I threw my suitcase on the bed I was claming for myself. "You stand there complaining about smoke smells. I'm gonna roll out and take a look around that creek where they supposedly found Johnson's clothes."

"You know what I don't get about this whole deal? Why are you the only one doing an investigation? It's been what? A year since he disappeared?"

I opened the sliding window to let in some Boston air. I didn't want to admit that Anthony was right about the cigarette smell, but it actually was starting to get to me, too.

"Anthony, as much as I love the bureau, you need to understand that they will keep anything quiet, if they need to. They will do anything to avoid a scandal or more dirt on our reputation. Malcolm Johnson was a fifteen-year veteran. His betrayal was the second D.C. scandal since that huge mess with Sebastian Rogers, a couple of years ago."

Anthony nodded. "Yeah, I remember that."

"You know they don't want more embarrassment. But I was never happy or satisfied with how quick the head office was willing to accept Johnson as dead, without even a body to prove it. If it was anyone else, the case would still be open."

Anthony threw the keys to our rented Jeep, which I caught readily.

"So you really believe he's still alive. This is gonna be a trip."

"I believe differently—I even think differently from most, Anthony."

"What do you mean?" he asked, following me out the door.

"Well, let's put it this way. When I was a kid, I used to spend a lot of time in the Frederick area. Things were a lot more rural then, at least certain parts or surrounding areas of Frederick County. My aunt had a small chicken farm. Whenever they would kill the mature birds, to get them ready for the market, I'd watch those fuckas dance around long after the head was chopped off. Somehow, I never believed that a chicken was dead if part of him was still moving. So whenever nobody was looking, I would take a stick and beat the hell out of that dancing bird."

Anthony was laughing as we jumped into the Jeep. "You were a sick kid."

"Hmm...maybe so," I admitted. "But I'm that same person today, sick or not. I'm not sure Johnson is still alive, and maybe I'll end up looking just as silly as I did, beating those dead chickens. But..." I started up the Jeep with a purr. "I'd rather be safe than sorry."

Kimberla

The next morning, I felt like crap. I still couldn't stop thinking and wondering where Jacob was. I also hadn't gotten much sleep. My nightmares were back again.

I actually put on extra makeup to hide my fatigue and worry lines. Lolita and I were in the computer lab, at FBI headquarters. We had confiscated the computers of David Rivers and Steven Michaels, but hadn't much luck getting a hold of Kaseem Soroco's. It pissed me off that his family and the Nigerian embassy were being so difficult where his case was concerned. But Kyte had promised he would work out the red tape, and help us get any evidence we needed. For now, we had to go on what we had.

"This is a hot mess," Lolita said.

I looked at the computer to see what she was talking about. She had a user name up, called Urban_Dreams.

"What is?" I asked.

"These sex names. I tell you, people are such freaka-zoids." She laughed. "Look at this."

I grabbed a chair and scooted up beside her.

"This dude, David Rivers, he had folders full of naked men. And look at these e-mails."

There was a mass amount of what obviously were group accounts with erotic stories and pictures, pretty much telling us that David Rivers was a freak himself.

"So you think we will find our killer somewhere in this freak-mess?" I asked, laughing.

"Maybe." Lolita shrugged. "A large percentage of murders are somehow connected to Net prowlers, you know."

I gave Lolita a puzzled look. "How do you know so much about this? You spend a lot of time online?"

"Not really." She nodded. "But I took a special training course a couple of years ago, on Internet crime."

"The CCI program?"

"Yep."

"Wow. I'm impressed," I stated. Actually I was slightly jealous. Well, not really jealous, but I had to grudgingly admit, my respect for Lolita Mason was growing. I didn't want to respect, or like, her. However, her professional credentials were undisputable.

"A year ago there was a very disturbing case I helped out with in L.A. A seventeen-year-old boy met this girl, or who he thought was a girl, on the Internet. He met her on one of these group message boards." Lolita motioned to the computer. "When they finally consented to meet face-to-face, come to find out his net boo was a he."

"Oh my God!" I exclaimed.

"When he threatened to expose the guy to what I'm guessing were their online communities of friends, he disappeared. We found him a month later, or what was left of him, scattered body parts at the killer's parents' vacation beach home in Palm Beach."

"That's horrible," I whispered.

I hadn't heard anything about that case, but my mind had images of the poor boy, and they weren't pretty.

"Kimberla, look at this!" Lolita grabbed my attention again.

She clicked on an e-mail from a user name on David Rivers's computer. She then moved to Steven Michaels, typed in the same name. Both came up. The user name was Catwomyn75. Both murder victims had associated in some form or another, with the same woman.

Lolita and I looked at each other and nodded. We finally had a match.

Jacob

The winds were high for a late summer morning, and so were the tides. To kill time before trying to meet Bailey Johnson, Anthony and I found ourselves outside observing the spot where Malcolm Johnson was supposed to have disappeared. I looked at the records, having grabbed them from the headquarters' reservoir, with all the in-and-out details of Johnson's case. A lot of things did not add up for me.

I walked over to the cliff edge, where Johnson's shoes were found. Anthony was already there.

"What you doing?" I asked him.

"Just doing some mental measuring," he said. "This is interesting."

"What is?"

"How did his shoes end up on top of these rocks, and yet his clothes…" He took ten hopping steps to the next pile of rocks. "How did they end up all the way over here? And if he jumped to his death, the way the report is speculating, his body would have ended up about ten feet from the beginning of the river water. It just doesn't make sense."

"That's true," I agreed. "And I'll tell you something else, Malcolm was not the type to get emotional to the point that he would worry about stripping before dipping to his death. He would be too scared that someone would see that fat, pale ass."

Anthony laughed, and then paused at the somber look on my face. "So he is alive?"

I didn't reply. Honestly, I wasn't sure if I thought Malcolm was still alive, or if he was just giving commands from the grave. One thing I did know, I wasn't going to rest until this uneasy premonition, stirring inside me, found a resting place, or better yet, an answer.

Kimberla

My kitchen smelled like chocolate.

Bree insisted on our fixing Toll House chocolate chip cookies for lunch, with extra chocolate bits, and being a secret chocoholic, I didn't resist too much.

Ignoring the mess, Bree, my girl Kendra, and I moaned, groaned, and snacked our way to sugar heaven.

"I can't believe you two have me stuffing myself like this," Kendra complained jokingly. "Each one of these cookies has to be at least five hundred calories. And I've had, um...how many?"

"Five! Dang, girl, you just had your quota of two days' worth of burgers. No wonder you're so big."

"Whatever," Kendra retorted. She rolled her eyes at my fit of giggles.

Bree looked a bit lost in our conversation at first. That's why I was very shocked and surprised, speechless, when she said, "Daddy says you're fat, Kimmy."

Kendra laughed and punched me in the arm.

"Did your daddy really say that?" she asked Bree.

"Yes." She nodded. "He told his friend Mr. Anthony that he misses your fat butt." She looked at me.

"Okay," I jumped in. "Enough!"

I could have slapped Kendra for that giggly look on her

face. Instead, I rolled my eyes and took my attention back to Bree.

"Why don't you go play outside for a little while, Bree? Kendra and I will clean up the cookie mess."

Predictably, she didn't protest at all. Bree grabbed a handful of extra cookies and bounced happily out the door.

"Well, she certainly is a bundle of energy," Kendra said.

"Yes, she is. I feel kind of bad that I haven't spent much time with her since Jacob and I broke up."

"Hmm…" Kendra observed me quietly and sipped her coffee. "My guess is you're missing him more than you miss playing mommy."

My eyes widened in surprise. "Kendra, that is a mean thing to say."

"Who's being mean? I was just making a comment."

"That is not a comment. That is a judgmental state-ment! As if I don't love Bree."

"Whoa!" Kendra drew back. "Calm down, Kimmy. I wasn't insinuating anything like that. It's not about Bree. She's a sweet little girl. It's about her daddy. The fact is, you love that man and you are too stubborn to admit it."

I didn't know why I was feeling so emotional. Yes, I did. But I didn't want to think about it. I wanted to cry, but I didn't. I fought too hard to keep my true feelings in check. To allow them to spill over now would be weak. Wouldn't it?

Suddenly my emotional balloon popped. I heard myself

confessing, "I'm so scared, Kendra..." I didn't realize tears were streaming down my cheeks.

Kendra put her coffee cup down and rushed to my side, taking my face in her hands. "What is wrong, girl? I know you've been holding something in for a while now. You know it's not healthy. Tell me what's wrong!"

What could I tell her? That monsters invaded my dreams every night? That the monsters were real, and they breathed and existed? Would I tell her that I can't love Jacob, that I can't give myself emotionally to anyone, because I don't trust any man?

As quickly as my emotional balloon deflated, it blew itself back up, and the large shield of protection I wore like a winter coat wrapped itself tightly back around me.

"Nothing," I said quietly. "I think I'm just tired."

"Huh? Oh no you don't! You always do this, Kimberla. Just once, stop trying to be so strong and just spit it out."

I ignored her. I got up and walked to the kitchen entranceway.

"We have some cleaning to do," I said. The sounds of Kendra's frustrated sighs echoed. Those, too, I ignored.

CHAPTER 17

Jacob

Bailey Hamilton lived in a wealthy, prominent housing development in north Boston. I wasn't sure what her reaction would be when we asked about her brother. But her reaction was what I actually wanted to judge. I wanted to see if she was indeed a sister in mourning. Perhaps my plans were a bit coldhearted. I just didn't see any other way. I wanted to see just how much she knew, if anything.

I assumed Malcolm's sister would be the reserved type. He himself had always been very arrogant. Kimberla had said he loved using his family's money and political connections as leverage to move up in rank and promotions with the bureau. Of course he wasn't so lucky since a promotion that he actually wanted had been given to Kimberla, and had been the sole reason for his deep-seated hatred for her.

The house was huge, but modest in comparison to others around it. The structure was obviously expensive.

"Rich bitches make me sick," Anthony said, sneering.

I laughed. "Don't hate. I wish I was so lucky."

"I'm not hating. But look at this mess." Anthony waved his hand around at the manicured lawn and redbrick semimansion. "You say it's just Hamilton and her husband. Why would they need all this? That's why working stiffs are always broke. The politicians are saving the dough for themselves."

We rang the bell and waited patiently. Opening the door was a short, older woman, dressed in servant clothes.

"Can I help you?" she asked.

"Yes. Is Mrs. Hamilton available?"

"Who can I tell her is calling?" the servant woman asked.

Before we could respond a voice said, "It's fine, Eleanor." A tall, handsome woman who looked to be around forty walked up to the door. "Can I help you?"

I extended my hand. "Are you Bailey Hamilton?"

"Yes, I am." Her eyebrows rose. "And again, what can I help you with?"

I was right. Bailey Hamilton seeped arrogance. It was in her tone, her stance, the way she held her head. I almost laughed out loud.

"I'm Rodney Green," I lied. "This is Charles Piers." I almost kicked Anthony when he coughed a bit. The fool needed to learn how to play along. "We are with an organization that seeks to honor fallen heroes. I understand you lost your brother recently. Malcolm Johnson?"

"Fallen heroes?" she repeated. "What is the name of your organization, Mr. Green?"

Before I could think of a response Bailey Hamilton

moved aside. A familiar face slid in front of hers. I felt the color drain from my own.

It was Malcolm Johnson, and there was nothing dead about him.

Lolita

There was something about the case that had Lolita mesmerized. With each similar murder, the original Soroco murder case was turning into a full-fledged serial situation.

Lolita looked through her information folders that profiled each of the murder victims. All black men, all seeming to have met their killer online. And now, all having talked to the same woman, if she was indeed a woman. Catwomyn75. Why did she pinpoint these men? What was it about them, other than having a fascination for the Internet, that made her want to kill them?

The telephone rang.

"Hello?" Lolita answered.

"Lolita, I found the information you wanted on that user name."

"Great!" She grabbed her notepad. "Give it to me now."

"You're in a hurry for this," Nigel Berry said.

Lolita had used Nigel when she worked in Los Angeles for source verification.

"Yes, I am. So stop stalling," she said with a laugh.

"Okay. The account was opened by Yvette Wilkins,

but the credit card used was a Visa, owned by Bianca Greenwich."

"What's the address?"

"Frederick, Maryland."

"Bingo!" Lolita exclaimed. Steven Michaels, the last murder victim, lived in Frederick.

"2234 Laurydale Drive."

"Great. Thanks, Nigel. Listen, is the owner of the card the same address?"

"No, it's Thurmont," Nigel answered.

"Where is Thurmont?"

"It's not far from Frederick. But there is one problem."

"What's that?"

Nigel gave a little cluck; that told her he was doing what he normally did, popping gum as he talked. It irritated her like crazy.

"Nigel!"

"Sorry." He laughed. "The problem is, when I checked the address for Bianca Greenwich on MapQuest, it's a rural field. There is no evidence of any homes in that area."

"Hmm…well, just give me the address, I'll make a trip and check it out for myself."

Jacob

Anthony and I stood there frozen, looking into the eyes of Malcolm Johnson.

"What do you want?" he said harshly.

He obviously didn't recognize me. I could feel Anthony nudging me, but nothing would come out of my mouth. Finally Anthony stepped in.

"Like we were saying, we wanted to get some information on Malcolm Johnson. We understood he was a celebrated FBI agent, and our company likes to recognize those who contribute to—"

"Come in," Malcolm said. Anthony stepped right through the door, but I hesitated.

"What's the problem?" Malcolm said, looking at me oddly.

I felt behind my back, making sure my gun was secure. It freaked me out that he didn't recognize me. There was something different about him. But mostly it was in his eyes.

"Ah," he said. "You've seen pictures of my brother and you think I'm him." He laughed. So did Bailey Hamilton.

"I wasn't aware that he had a brother," I said.

"Eleanor, get our guests some...coffee?" Bailey Hamilton looked at me and Anthony.

"That's fine," I said thankfully.

We walked to the sitting room that was off the living room. "So what's your name?" I asked Malcolm's look-alike.

"Miles. I'm Miles Johnson. And yes, Malcolm was my twin."

"I wasn't aware that Malcolm had a twin. We were told he only had a half sister."

"Why would you know? You're just a reporter, right?" Miles gave me and Anthony a meaningful look.

"Of course," I said. "I'm just saying that our sources are pretty good in grabbing information. They gave us the impression that we had everything on Mr. Johnson."

"Exactly how much information do you need on a dead man, just to give an award?" Bailey Johnson asked suspiciously. "Who are you really?"

I could have kicked myself. In all honesty, Anthony and I had just jumped into this situation without thinking it out clearly. Certainly without thinking that we would be confronted with a brother and a sister.

"We told you who we were," Anthony said.

"And you're lying." Miles Johnson looked directly at me. "Are you Agent White?"

He knew who I was! I jumped up, grabbing my gun from behind me in one step, and aimed it at both Miles Johnson and Bailey Hamilton. Anthony watched anxiously.

Miles laughed, and put his hands up in mock surrender. "I must say, Agent White, we aren't used to guests being so rude."

"Bullshit. You knew who I was from the start."

"On the contrary." Miles smirked. "You knew who you were from the start. Now why don't we stop playing these games and you tell us what the hell you are really looking for?"

"Someone attacked two of our agents. We are trying to find out who's responsible."

"And you think our brother has something to do with this?" Miles asked.

"You tell me."

"I tell you what." Miles motioned as if he were going to come closer to me. I cocked the hammer. He laughed. "I think maybe you guys should stick around awhile. Maybe you'll find something."

"Stick around?" I asked curiously.

Anthony gasped. I looked down to see what was wrong and saw a gun pointed at the back of his head. A second later I felt one sticking in my back. The only word that could come out of my mouth was "Damn…"

CHAPTER 18

Kimberla

The weather was sunny and cheery the next morning. Bree's face was happy and serene when I dropped her off. It amazed me what little effort it took to please children. All they wanted was a little love and attention. Actually that's all I really had wanted when I was a child, too.

"Are you going to get me next weekend?" she asked as we walked to her and Jacob's condo. Jacob's babysitter had already opened the door to greet us.

"I sure will," I said. "Your daddy will be back in a couple of days, though."

I stooped down in front of her with my arms outstretched. Bree came into them and we paused for a big hug.

When she pulled back, she asked quietly, "Kimmy, are you and my daddy ever gonna get married?"

Oh Lawd! I thought. She was as blunt and persistent as her father. The thing was, I couldn't bring myself to break her little girl's heart. It was obvious she had high hopes on me becoming her new mama.

"Bree, I really can't answer that," I finally said.

"Why not? Don't you love each other? My teacher told us last year that when people love each other, they get married."

"True. But, sweetie, sometimes it's a bit more complicated than that."

Bree looked at me inquisitively and bent her head to the side. "I guess that's grown folks business, right?"

I laughed. "Yes, it's grown folks business. When you're a grown up, I think you'll understand more." I hugged her again, and then kissed her on her cheeks. "I love you, Miss Bree."

"I love you, too," Bree shouted. "Next weekend. Don't forget!"

"I won't."

I was smiling as I walked to get in my car. Bree always had a way of cheering me up.

I sighed contentedly. I needed to meet with Lolita. She had gotten some information on the user names and we were going to take a trip to Thurmont and Frederick, she said. Hopefully we would get to talk to someone.

As I started my car, my pager beeped. I looked down at the screen. It was Kyte. That surprised me and I couldn't help but wonder what he wanted. Kyte had just told me the day before that he was going to lay off and just let Lolita and me do our job. I guess he changed that idea quickly. I had no choice but to call him back.

"What's up, Chief?" I asked with a saccharine tone to

my voice. I knew I was bordering a bit on insubordination, but Kyte had a tendency to get worrisome.

"Hey. Kimberla, have you heard from Jacob?"

"Jacob? Not today. I had his daughter all weekend. I just dropped her off."

"Did he tell you where he was going?"

"Um… Kyte, why all the questions? Jacob is on vacation, you know that. He hasn't been reassigned, has he?"

Kyte's voice sounded worried. "No, he hasn't and that's the problem. He got a hold of some classified information. I need to know what he wanted it for. Especially since he hasn't been reassigned."

"What information?" I asked.

"Don't worry about it—"

"Kyte, come on now! You can't call me with this and expect me not to be concerned. What information did Jacob get a hold of?"

"Okay. He got files concerning Malcolm Johnson's disappearance."

Malcolm Johnson. The sound of his name started my heart beating rapidly. I didn't like the way this was sounding at all.

"His disappearance? You mean his death, right?"

"No, Kimberla," Kyte said slowly. "About Malcolm… um…"

"What about him? What about Malcolm, Kyte?"

"He's still alive," Kyte said somberly.

"What?"

Oh my God! my mind was screaming. Where the hell was Jacob!

Jacob

What started out as a curious inquiry was now a very serious situation. Anthony and I had been taken by car to some old house about an hour away. At least the drive felt like an hour.

"Sit down!" a tall, bald, green-eyed guy said. He pushed Anthony and then me into the scantily furnished house.

"Why are we here?" I asked him. I sat down in the two-posted chair that sat back-to-back with Anthony's.

"That's a question you need to be answering, don't you think? Nobody told you to bring your ass to Boston. Now put your arms behind the chair." He roughly yanked my arms behind me.

Another man was already tying Anthony up. I flexed my fingers a little once I was tied.

With both hands and feet bound, Baldie gave us one last hostile glance before leaving and closing the door behind him.

"Great!" Anthony fumed. "What the hell have you gotten us into?"

"Me? Man, how was I supposed to know this was going to happen? Bailey is a high-society wife of a senator. Who would think she was a crook along with her brother?"

"Brothers, you mean. They're twins, remember?"

I breathed in deeply. "Okay, there is no point in our complaining about who is right and who is wrong." I leaned close to him.

"What?" Anthony said, jerking back.

"Nigga, I'm not trying to kiss you!" I whispered. "I just realized they may be listening in on us. We need to figure out a way to get out of here."

"And how do you suggest we do that, Mr. Know-It-All?"

I ignored his smart remarks. Both of us were stressed out. I moved my fingers back and forth, fighting to get in the inside cuff of my suit coat. The small knife I always kept there slid into the palm of my hand.

"What are you doing?" Anthony asked loudly.

"Shh!"

With the knife in my hand, I started sliding it back and forth over the rope. It was rather awkward, since the blade was so small. Just then, the front door opened.

"I hope you gentlemen are comfortable." It was Miles Johnson.

Looking at him now, I could see more clearly that he was not Malcolm Johnson. The resemblance was uncanny but the difference, especially in the body size, the height, and the slimness of the face, was pretty obvious.

I pushed my pocketknife back in the sleeve of my jacket.

"Why did you bring us here?" Anthony asked.

"You have no authority to ask questions. I ask the questions," he responded.

Miles was seriously starting to piss me off.

"Do you know how much trouble you are in for abducting a federal agent?" I asked between clenched teeth.

"Agent White, surely you are joking? Federal agent? The FBI is a joke. They don't give a damn what happens to you. Their biggest concern is silence. Don't you know that by now?"

What the heck was he talking about?

"And what's that supposed to mean?" I asked.

"Let me put it this way. Why do you think they let my brother get away? You worked on the Michael Riley case, if I have my facts correct. Do you really think your people are on the up-and-up?"

"Well, I know your brother was not on the up-and-up. He was a damn crook and a shame to his badge. He got exactly what he deserved!"

Miles sat quietly, listening to me rant. He pulled a cigarette from a pack and lit it. He then walked over to me and blew the smoke in my face. I resisted the urge to cough, and challenged him eye-to-eye.

"You think he got what he deserved, do you?"

"Hell yeah," I said. "He was a dirty agent. He was a crook, just like you."

I saw from the corner of my eye his lit cigarette moving toward my face. I couldn't move fast enough as he pushed it into my cheek.

"Ugghh!" I exclaimed. "You muthafuck!"

"Yeah, that's me, and half the dirty agents you work for, too."

My body shook from the burning pain in my face. Damn, I thought, couldn't he have picked any other place to use as his ashtray? I looked at him with a murderous expression. He looked back at me, smiling.

"Don't worry," he mocked. "You'll be a pretty corpse regardless."

"Fuck you!" I spat back.

"So are you going to kill us?" Anthony asked in panic.

"I don't know. Why don't you tell me why you two really came to see my sister?"

"None of your damn business," I said quietly.

Miles didn't bother to relight his cigarette. This time he put the mouth of his gun between my eyes and cocked it.

"If I blow your damn head off there's not a damn thing they could do to make sure you lie pretty in your casket. How about that, smart-ass?"

"Wait!" Anthony interjected. "We wanted to find out what she knew, if anything, about your brother."

"Why is that?"

"Because an agent was killed and one attacked, about a month ago. Jacob here thought he had seen your brother in passing."

I wanted to kill Anthony myself for running his big mouth. "Shut the hell up, man!"

"Ohhhh." Miles laughed. "So you came because you think my brother has something to do with it? Yes, you said that before at the house. And what makes you think he had something to do with it?"

"You would know the answer to that."

Miles's eyes came back to me. "I would?"

"Yeah, you should know. But he's supposed to be dead, right?"

Miles flopped back in his chair, relit his tobacco stick, and took a deep draw.

"You know he's not dead, Agent White. That's a lie fabricated by your people. And guess what? Until I find out where you have him hidden, you two aren't going no damn where. Let's just call it an even trade."

Anthony and I looked at each other in confusion. Everything we had thought we knew about Malcolm just got far, far more confusing.

CHAPTER 19

Kimberla

Lolita would just have to wait. I paced back and forth in Kyte's office, waiting for him to show up and spit out whatever it was he was hiding all this time. I was so angry with him; so angry with the bureau for putting me, and now Jacob, in unnecessary danger. I was so pissed that Micah was dead; pissed at them pretending not to know anything about who could have been the cause of it. All along they knew Malcolm Johnson was alive.

The door opened. Kyte looked at me guiltily. I put my hand up as he began to speak.

"I don't want to hear any bullshit excuses. I just want to know why," I said.

"Kimberla, come sit down."

"No!" I almost shouted. "He's alive? All this time you knew Malcolm was alive and you didn't say anything?"

"There was reason for that, Kimberla. You know how things are run as well as I do. As much as I wanted to tell you, I couldn't. Not yet."

"And where is he now?"

Kyte sat down quietly behind his desk. He rubbed his hands over his face as if he was tired.

"That's the problem," he finally said. "We don't know where he is."

"But you did know?" I pressed.

"Yes."

"And you conveniently decided not to tell me?"

"It wasn't like that. We had him under protective custody for the past year. He didn't turn up missing until the night you and Micah were attacked."

Suddenly, so out of character for me, I started crying. "And you didn't tell me? God, Kyte! How could you? How—"

"Kimberla, this is far deeper than what you can imagine. We had to keep him under protective care. Malcolm wasn't working alone when that drug case went foul in New York. He was to testify against some major heads of the bureau. Don't you understand? It was vital that we fake his death and keep this under wraps!"

"And what about me? What about the fact that you knew if he ever got out he would come after me? He had sworn vengeance from the very start. You knew that. What about Micah? I had to—" I got choked up. Choked on my own shock of what Kyte was telling me. The simple betrayal of what I had always looked at as my team, my family.

"I had to look Micah's mother in the eye, and tell her that I didn't know why her son was dead."

"I'm sorry, Kimberla," Kyte said sadly. "I miss Micah

as much as you do. He was a loyal agent, and a fantastic person. You know if there was anything I could have done to avoid this, I would have."

I was out of energy. It seemed as if everything I ever believed, everything I ever trusted concerning being an FBI agent, was a farce and a lie. A joke, where getting to the big guys was more important than protecting those who dedicated their life to justice.

Kyte walked over, putting his arm around my shoulder.

"Kimberla, I know you're disappointed and hurt. Trust me, we are doing everything we can to find Johnson. We do suspect that he was responsible for Micah's death and your attack. That gives us even more reasons to push as hard as we can to get him off the street."

I looked at him. "And in the meanwhile, I just have to watch my back?" I shook my head. "I'm done, Kyte."

"What do you mean you're done?"

I jumped up. "I mean exactly what I just said. I'm done. I risk my life. I give my all to do the best damn job I can. What do I get in way of thanks? A demotion, my life at risk, I lose my partner and friend. I quit."

I reached to take my badge out and handed it to him. Kyte shook his head in refusal.

"Hell no, you can't quit. Kimberla, we need you. You're one of the best agents I have. Besides, quitting is not going to make you any safer."

"Oh, I'm supposed to be safe now?" I said with a humorless laugh.

"No, but I know you aren't a quitter, and Lolita is depending on you. We are going to watch out for you, both of you. But I know you, Kimberla. I know you want and need to solve the Soroco case. If for no other reason, your own ego and pride."

"No, that's you, that's your pride, Kyte."

"Kimberla, please," he pleaded. He pushed my badge back at me. "If after this case you decide you really are done, I'll accept your resignation with no argument. But don't let emotion change who you are. This is not you."

Was I a quitter? I didn't know anymore. Everything I thought I knew about my life, about who I was and what was important to me, seemed to be vanishing. I walked over to the scenic window that I had always loved about Kyte's office. People walked to and fro as if no worry plagued them. I wished I was them.

"What about Jacob?" I asked. My back was still to Kyte.

"We have no idea where he is. All I know is he got a hold of Malcolm's files. I'm worried about what he knows, and I'm worried about what he may be trying to do about it."

I turned around. My face was bleak. "And you want me to find him?"

"No, I want you find this Catwomyn killer. I want you to do what you do best. If Jacob contacts you, I want you to call me immediately. We can't risk him."

I almost laughed at Kyte's words. *We can't risk him.* Everything was at risk now. I had no idea where Jacob was.

I had no idea when, or if, my archenemy could be ready to stick a knife in my back. All I could do was laugh.

The raspberry iced tea was cool running down my throat. I needed it for more than thirst. My mind was in shambles. I tried hard to pay attention to Lolita speaking. I felt bad that I wasn't giving this case the attention it deserved and she seemed to be doing all the investigative work. I wondered again where Jacob was. He hadn't called, and he knew Bree had been with me for the weekend. It wasn't like him to not even check up on her.

"So when I went to Yvette Wilkins's house, nobody was there, right? I go to her so-called aunt's house in Thurmont, and she's dead. So then I drove over to Jacob's house and we had hot sex on the beach—"

"Huh?" I blinked.

"I thought that would get your attention." Lolita smirked.

"Whatever, bitch!"

"Oh, don't call me a bitch. I'm trying to talk to you and you're in la-la land. The only thing you wake up for is your worry that someone is gonna be boning Jacob besides you."

"I hope you don't think that was funny!"

I was steamed. I fumbled with my silverware, took a big gulp of my iced tea, and fought to calm my nerves.

"You weren't even listening to me," Lolita reprimanded me. "Grrr...listen, Kimberla, I wanted to work with you because your reputation has no limits. I have wanted to work with you for a long time. But ever since we started this case you've seemed totally uninterested. I don't know if it's simply because you don't want to work with me, or you have something else on your mind. There are lives involved here. The longer we wait and fool around, ignoring vital information and moving at a snail's pace as if it's not important, the more people will be killed. It's not fair to them, and it's not fair to me. I, for one, intend to do the best job that I can, and as an agent, if you don't feel you can do the same thing, you shouldn't be one!"

My soup seemed to have gotten cold and bland. I stirred my spoon around in it, looking for a response to Lolita that honestly wouldn't come. The truth is, she was right. I had always taken pride myself in being the best at my job. What had happened to me?

"Kimberla!" a voice shouted out.

Both Lolita and I turned toward it. It was Kendra. She walked over, smiling and waving.

"Hey, girl," I said. I got up and gave her a hug. "What are you doing here? I thought you had surgery today."

She pulled out a chair and flopped down in it, taking a deep breath.

"Whoa!" she breathed, as if tired. "I did, but it's been postponed. I swear I love my job, but sometimes it can get so aggravating." Kendra put her hands up and smacked them back on the table as if she had just finished a tiresome recital. She suddenly noticed Lolita. "Oh. Hello." She smiled.

"Girl, you so crazy." I laughed. "This is my partner, Lolita. Lolita, this is Kendra."

Both ladies smiled politely and extended their hands.

"Nice to meet you, Lolita. I've heard a lot about you."

I kicked Kendra and made a face at her.

"I'm sure you have," Lolita said with a smirk. "So, you're a doctor?"

"Yes, I am. I would ask what you do, but I already know!" Kendra winked.

Just then our waitress showed up with a pitcher of water to refill our glasses, and asked Kendra if she would like to order.

"I'll take the broccoli and cheese soup, and an ice tea, please," she said.

"That's a beautiful, odd bracelet you have, Kendra," Lolita noted.

We all looked at her wrist. The bracelet was a charm that Kendra had worn for years, given to her by her late husband.

"Thank you," she said, touching it. "It was a gift."

"Well, can I see it?" Lolita asked.

"Why?" I interjected.

"No reason." Lolita gave a little laugh. "I just like exotic jewelry. I haven't seen a charm bracelet like that in ages. What type of charms are they?" she asked.

Kendra pushed her arm at Lolita. She had a tight and what I recognized, being that I had known her since forever, as an annoyed expression on her face.

"It's exquisite," Lolita said sweetly.

"Um…thank you."

There was a tense silence that followed. I was pissed and very relieved when the waitress finally showed up with Kendra's order.

"You got the same kind of soup I have," Lolita said. She took a spoonful of her own. "It's delicious!"

CHAPTER 20

Catwomyn75

She loved darkness. She loved when the sun was down and the stars danced a quiet waltz in the sky. That's how her grandfather used to describe the night. He considered himself somewhat of a poet. She shared his feelings. The night gave her freedom. She felt trapped, normally, inside an avalanche of pain.

During the day she had to pretend; she had to smile on cue and laugh when others did. She had to live a farce that was slowly suffocating her.

She hadn't gotten on her computer in a while. She still cringed inside when she thought about her actions with Steven Michaels, and the fact that she had enjoyed what he did to her. Men weren't meant to be enjoyed. That desire, or so she thought, had died with her the night she'd caught her dog of a husband making love to a man.

The phone rang. She was almost too tired to get it. Any outside disturbance always disrupted her peace time.

"Hello?"

"Someone came around looking for you."

She frowned. "Looking for me? Who was it?"

"I don't know. It was some policewoman."

She felt panic. Why would anyone, especially the police, be looking for her? She had covered her tracks so well.

"What did she say? You didn't tell her my name, did you?" she almost shouted.

"Calm down! No, I didn't tell her your real name. What's all the secrecy about anyhow?"

"There is no secrecy... I just wondered. Anyhow, tell me if she comes back."

"Will do."

She hung up. A feeling of anxiety came over her. They were getting close to her. Someone suspected her.

She sat on the edge of her bed and began to rock. Faster and faster she rocked. It all flew out the window, the peace. It vanished.

"Why do people always fuck with me!" she shouted. "Why can't they just leave me the hell alone?"

She needed something, something that always made her feel better. She got up, walked over to her computer desk, and signed on.

Jacob

The longer we heard no word from Miles, the more nervous I got. I wasn't as bad as Anthony. He had bitched and complained about being hungry for the last four hours. I couldn't much blame him. Anthony was from a different breed than me.

All this time sitting and waiting had my mind going back to all the situations that had happened in my life for the past few years. Losing my wife had left a permanent mark on my soul. Falling in love with Kimberla had left another one. Losing her love, the love she never really announced, ripped a hole in me. But losing the opportunity to make her take me back was a mark I wasn't going to allow to be written. If I ever got that chance, that is.

"You would think the bastard would at least give us a damn cup of water," Anthony complained.

I said nothing.

"Do you hear me, Jacob? This is crazy, man!"

"No," I said, feeling annoyed. "What's crazy is you can't shut your damn trap."

"What's crazy is that you pulled us into this shit and now you're sitting there not saying anything and I'm hungry and thirsty and I'm not trying to die no time soon!"

I knew he was right. I felt so guilty for taking the chance I took, not necessarily with my own life, but with Anthony's. I didn't want to tell him that I suspected Miles had no intention of letting us out alive. Or worse still, there was no way in the world he would get what he wanted: his brother in the place of us. That's not how the Feds operated. *We don't negotiate with criminals.* That was the golden rule with the current administration, and the FBI was simply a reflection of this.

"I know, and I'm sorry, Anthony," I said sadly. "I don't think we're going to be in here much longer."

"I don't know if that's a good thing or a bad thing..."
I swallowed deeply. I didn't know, either.

Kimberla

The next morning, Lolita and I met early to take a trip
to see, and hopefully speak with Bianca Greenwich.

Anthony Hamilton caressed me with his song. I lay
back against the leather seat of Lolita's car and thought
about happier days. Believe it or not, the happy days were
the ones in New York, when Jacob and I had first started
our, um...affair. Actually I didn't know how to describe
what we had. I don't know what it was about me. I had a
tendency to be attracted to strong people, someone who
would fight me back, challenge me, I guess one would call
it. In the beginning, that's what Jacob did. He challenged
me sexually, emotionally, mentally. And he wasn't saying
I love you.

Who was I kidding? I knew he loved me. I knew he was
still a strong man. I'm the one who had the problem.
When someone says they love you, it obligates you to say
it back. That wouldn't be a problem for me, if I actually
didn't love him back, but I did. That put other obligations
on the table. That meant I had to open up so many deep,
dark secrets that I couldn't, I just couldn't! Now I didn't
even know where he was. It wasn't like him to not call. I
just knew something was wrong. And I knew that
Malcolm Johnson had something to do with it.

"Are you feeling okay, Kimberla?" Lolita asked.

"Of course I am. Why?"

"You're just so quiet. We should be in Thurmont in a few minutes. I really didn't trust what that niece said."

"Why didn't you take a search warrant before you went over there?" I pondered.

"First of all, I wanted to be sure I had the right house, person, and all my T's crossed. Second, what would be the basis of my search warrant? We don't know if Bianca had anything to do with these killings. We don't know if Catwomyn75 had anything to do with them. All we really know is she had contact with all these murder victims. Could have helped a lot if you had gone with me, though," she said sarcastically.

"Well, I didn't, so deal with it."

Lolita giggled. I was not gonna let her get to me today, so I ignored it.

"Hey, how is your doctor friend doing?"

"Kendra is fine." I jumped when I remembered what I wanted to ask her. "Hey! What was up with you yesterday, anyhow?"

"I was waiting for you to ask that," Lolita said with a laugh. "I just found her charm bracelet interesting."

"I would say you found it more than interesting. Not that I know you all that well, but you were downright weird, and rude."

"Not rude. I just found it odd…"

"Found what odd?" I quizzed.

"Okay, don't get mad when I ask you this, all right?"

When I didn't respond, she continued.

"Do you remember that charm we found at the Michaels's murder scene?"

"Yes. *What* about it?"

"Don't get that tone. Like I said, I just found it curious. A couple of the charms on Kendra's bracelet looked exactly like—"

Oh no, she wasn't! I just knew damn well she wasn't trying to accuse Kendra.

"How are you gonna tell me not to get angry? You're trying to call my friend a killer? I've known Kendra all my life. She is my oldest and dearest friend!"

"I'm not trying to accuse her of anything. I just noticed the charms, is all. Don't get your panties in a bunch."

Lolita turned a corner and had to stomp on the brakes to avoid collision with a tractor.

"Damn hicks!" she shouted.

"Forget that. Pay attention to the road and you won't have to worry about hicks. And if you aren't accusing Kendra, why bring up her bracelet? A zillion people could have that type of charm."

"Hmm," she said, looking thoughtful. "You're right. But then again, I have only seen her with it. Where did she get that bracelet from anyhow?"

"Her husband, years ago!"

"I didn't realize she was married. I didn't see a ring on her finger."

"Maybe because her husband passed away, Lolita."

This conversation was getting old. I could appreciate an agent who checked out every nook and corner, but I had known Kendra for so long. I felt insulted.

"Wow!" Lolita exclaimed. "How did he die?"

"I'm not answering any more of your ridiculous questions. Don't you think I would know if my best friend was capable of being involved in something criminal? She is an educated, beautiful person. You are wrong!"

"I've been told that a time or two. Normally I was right. But, Kimberla, as I said before, I am not accusing Kendra of anything. I think you should go to the lab and take a second look at that charm, though."

"No, thank you. You are wrong to even question this."

"Listen—"

I swung around angrily. "No, you listen. My girl has been through a lot. So she has a bracelet with freakin' charms on it. That gives you no right to ask these questions. I don't want to talk about this anymore."

"Okay. My bad. Anyhow, we're here."

I swallowed convulsively and counted to ten. I wasn't going to think about what she was suggesting. I was good at erasing bullshit from my mind. So her words were officially erased. I wasn't going to let myself be upset about them.

A minute later Lolita pulled her car in front of an old house. It looked empty. We looked at each other, surprised.

"Are you sure this is the right place?" I asked.

She nodded. "It has to be. Hand me that map in my glove compartment."

After I gave her the map she looked it over. Back and forth, upside down. She then put it down and gave a "whatever" sigh. "It's the right house. I don't know, maybe she's eccentric or something. This is exactly the address and information I got from Visa."

"Hmm…well, let's check it out. After all, you couldn't be *wrong*, now, could you?" I said smartly.

She smiled demurely. "You got that right, chickadee."

CHAPTER 21

Jacob

Anthony had fallen asleep in his little wooden chair. Both of us had stayed awake all night, and sleep still had not caught up with me, even though it had to be close to noon.

My mouth felt like sandpaper. I was okay with not having any food. But after a day and a half of no water, I was about to start whining like Anthony. What the hell was going on?

I turned my head around and looked at the shiny, sharp instrument that was my useless knife. I really had screwed that one up. My face hurt. I had to find a way out of this fucked-up situation. And I had to pee! *Ugh,* I thought.

I jumped when the front door cracked open. Miles walked in, not looking very happy at all.

"Wow," I teased. "I can't believe you decided to pay your prisoners a visit."

He walked around the room slowly, came up to the window, and pulled down the half-ripped shade. "You know, White... I'm getting real sick of your smart mouth."

"Pardon me." I kept my eyes right on him, and smiled when he looked at me. That made my face hurt worse.

"Trust that you won't receive any pardon from me."

Miles walked over to the chair he had sat in hours before, facing us. "I talked to your people."

That got my attention! "Do they know where we are?"

"Of course not, idiot. You know, I'm very disappointed."

I looked at him under hooded eyelids. "Oh, really? And why is that?"

Miles had his gun in his hand. He was blowing on it, shining it up as if it was his most prized possession. I knew it wasn't, of course. We were his most prized possessions, at least at the moment we were.

"Why are you disappointed? Did you tell them you have us? What did they say?" I pressed.

"Yes, they know you are here. And actually they had a lot to say, but unfortunately for you..." Miles lifted his gun and pointed it at me. I closed my eyes as he cocked it.

A loud popping sound made me jump, but I didn't feel any pain. I opened my eyes. My body was shaking. Miles's gun was smoking at the tip. I felt confused for a moment, until I looked over behind me at Anthony. His eyes were still closed, but I knew at that moment, and at the blood rolling down his face out of the bullet hole between his eyes, his eyes were never going to open again.

"Oh my God! What the hell! Why did you do that?"

He walked over to me and put the hot tip of his pistol against the burn mark on my cheek. I was so in shock and disbelief over what had just happened to Anthony, I couldn't even feel pain.

"Because, you piece of pig trash," Miles slurred out, "they told me my brother was dead. They told me there could be no exchange." He dug the gun harder in my face. "Now they got one more chance to save one of you sorry pieces of—" Miles choked, and then took a deep breath, trying to compose himself. He held the gun to my face, then pulled back to make a call on his cell.

"You tell them what just happened. Tell them they have one more live agent, and only one more chance, because if they don't have my brother here in twenty-four hours, you're next."

I looked at the madman and shook my head.

"Tell them!" he screamed. His gun dug in my face again.

"Federal Bureau of Investigation. How can I direct your call?"

I looked at Miles questioningly. "I don't even know who to ask for," I said in a shaky voice.

"Ask for your boss. You're supposed to be smart, pig!"

"How can I direct your call?" the operator asked again.

I cleared my throat. "This is Agent Jacob White. I need to speak with Captain Kyte Williams."

"Just a moment, please."

I looked up at Miles Johnson. He was smiling, and then the psycho fool started whistling.

Kimberla

It didn't make any sense. The house was a hollow shell, empty. The walls of the house were covered with chipped white paint. Underneath the dull white was the blue hue over old, almost decayed walls. It made even less sense when someone knocked on the screen door, calling out to us.

"Hello? Who's in there? Who are you looking for?" the person hollered.

Lolita and I turned toward the voice at the same time and walked outside. A woman, looking to be in her seventies or eighties, looked back at us.

"Hi," she said again. She gave us a big, bright smile.

"Hello, there," I said back. "We're looking for Bianca Greenwich."

"Bianca? Chile, nobody lives here. Ain't nobody lived here for six months."

Lolita and I looked at each other, puzzled.

"Did she move? Do you know where she is?" Lolita asked.

The old woman walked over to us with the aid of a cane. "Well, I reckon she lives with the Lord now, chile. She passed on six months ago."

"She's dead?" we asked at the same time.

"Surely is. I was wonderin' who y'all was. Nobody comes around here much."

Lolita shook her head. "No, I mean— What about her family? Do you know anything about her family?"

"Well," the old woman said, scratching her head. "She

had a niece. Purty lil' thing. I never see her around no more. I always wondered why she didn't do sumpin' to this house."

"Do you know the niece's name?"

I looked at Lolita, curious at her question. She knew the niece's name. I wondered why she asked that.

"Naw." The old lady nodded. "I can't say that I do. Funny thing was, Ms. Bianca just called her 'niece.'" She laughed. "Ain't that a blast? She was a good woman. Yep, she surely was."

The house had an odor to it. It was actually making my stomach feel unsettled. I wanted to get out of there.

"Well, thank you, Ms....?"

"Salem. My name is Elizabeth Salem."

I smiled and shook her hand. "Well, I guess we better be going," I said to Lolita.

"Wait a minute," Lolita said, to stall. "Do you remember what her niece looks like? Can you describe her?"

"No." Ms. Salem shook her head again. "She was a purty brown thing. Like her aunty. She didn't come around much." She cocked her head and gave us an interested look. "She ain't in no trouble or nuttin', is she?"

"No, no," Lolita said. "Um...thanks again for your help."

Quiet puzzlement filled the air on the ride back to D.C. Obviously Yvette Wilkins was fabricating that Bianca Greenwich was still alive.

"I don't think that's her name," Lolita said.

"Who do you mean? Ms. Salem?"

"No." She nodded. "Yvette Wilkins. I had the card traced. She's rented vehicles, and she has an Internet service account in her deceased aunt's name. She is trying to cover her tracks."

I agreed. "She doesn't want anyone to know *something*."

"Something? Naw. Kimberla, I think we have our killer."

Lolita paused at the light. She looked to be in deep thought.

"You may be right," I said. "But it doesn't matter if we can't find out who she really is."

"True."

My cell phone rang.

"Kimmy..."

"Hey, Kyte!"

"I have some news for you about Jacob," he said solemnly.

"What kind of news?"

My face dropped; my demeanor changed from that of a curious investigating agent to a scared, concerned woman in love.

Lolita noticed my change in mood and the tone of my voice.

She must also have noticed my hand shaking as I held my phone. She mouthed silently, "What's wrong?"

I shook my head violently.

"Kimberla, he's been abducted. He must have been trying to investigate on his own this Malcolm crap." Kyte sighed.

I cried. My world was spinning.

"It's just a big mess," he said.

It was more than a mess. I knew that Jacob had gone to protect me. Even after the way I had been treating him. He risked his life to find closure for me. The tears were covering my face. They wouldn't stop.

"Okay, okay." I tried to catch my breath. "Now what?"

"Kimberla, listen, there's something else. He had someone with him. Someone named Anthony. Do you know him?"

"Of course I do. When we talked he said he and Anthony had to take care of some business. He didn't tell me what it was, though."

My breath caught at the next news.

"Jacob told me they killed him. And the abductor told us if we don't produce Malcolm within the next twenty-four hours, Jacob is next."

"Next? What do you mean next? Kyte!"

"You know what I mean." Kyte's voice softened. "Sweetie, I'm so sorry. Trust me we're going to do everything we can to get him back. I need your help, though. I need you to tell me everything you know about Anthony. What's his last name?"

"Lo-Lowery. Anthony Lowery. He used to work with Jacob when he was on the state force."

My voice cracked on every syllable. I felt sick and dizzy. But even so, I was thinking of a way to save Jacob.

"Kyte, I have an idea. I think I can find out where they went. I'm on my way to your office now!"

CHAPTER 22

Kimberla

Kyte should have known he couldn't stop me; neither could Lolita, with all her commonsense reasoning. After hearing my half of the conversation with Kyte over the phone, she pretty much insisted on knowing from both of us exactly what was going on. I didn't care. All I cared about was finding my man and letting him know how much I loved and needed him.

It's the little things, the little things that happen in life that teach you what's really important. Jacob went out on a limb for me. He had put himself in the way of danger because he thought I was in danger. I couldn't let him down now.

As soon as Kyte and I found out that Jacob and Anthony had gone to Boston, I was on the first flight there. Kyte said that whoever it was that had Jacob would recognize me. He had it twisted, or either he forgot the reason they called me Chameleon.

I had taken a quick flight, and by 8:00 p.m. I was in Boston. After rushing from the airport and finding a hotel, I sat, semiexhausted, on my hotel bed. I couldn't allow the physical to affect my mental. I wouldn't. Time was not on my side in this case.

My cell phone rang constantly. I knew it was Kyte. Even though I had not told him what I was going to do, he knew. He had to know. I figured he already had a team of FBI "let's go rescue this insane woman" already on the way to Boston to get me.

I stripped off my clothes, and took my disguise out of my suitcase. I paused to look over the records of Malcolm Johnson's disappearance, which Kyte told me Jacob had gotten. Hopefully it would give me an idea of where he could be. I dressed in thug clothing. I had on baggy pants to hide my slight, very slight, curves, and a big baggy Polo shirt. Of course I had to tie down my boobs. I wasn't the biggest in that department, but I did have something. Last but not least, I pulled out my fast-drying putty solution that would help me alter my facial features to appear more masculine. I concentrated on the shape of my nose and cheekbones. Finally satisfied with my disguise, I grabbed the slip of paper that I had written down the address of Bailey Hamilton on and headed out the door.

Lolita

Lolita was worried. She tried not to show it while she was with Kimberla. That woman already had jealousy issues. But she was really worried about Jacob. She was also puzzled. What dirty agent could be so important to nail that the bureau would allow this Malcolm Johnson to avoid prosecution and jail time? She always tried not to question her superiors. But in this case, she couldn't help it.

Oh well, she thought. She needed to get her mind off those things, and back on the investigation. Kimberla had skipped town. Even though Lolita knew Kimberla didn't like her very much, she hoped her partner wasn't biting off more than she could chew. To be honest, if she didn't have some very important information she needed to look into, she would have gone with Kimberla herself. Jacob was a great person; sexy, too. And she surely didn't want anything bad to happen to him. At the moment, it appeared that her old lover and friend was in the lion's pit.

Lolita shook off her daydreaming, determined to get her mind back on task. She had decided to go to the public library and look up old news articles on Kimberla's friend Kendra Gray. She wasn't sure what it was. For sure, Kendra seemed like a nice person. But also for sure, as Lolita knew jewelry, she knew those charms were not typical. Kimberla didn't know that Lolita's father had been a jewelry specialist, and ran and operated his own shop since she was ten years old. She had worked and learned everything he knew. The charm that was found at the hotel scene was crafted, unique, and it was just like Kendra Gray's. There was something there, and Lolita wanted to find out what it was.

She typed in Kendra's name. Kendra was a respected doctor, had graduated top of her class from both college and med school. Hmm...interesting, Lolita thought. Smart chick. Lolita scanned down farther, to a link about the sudden death of Kendra's husband. What she saw shocked her: *death caused by sudden heart failure.*

It was the exact cause of death as that of the murder victims.

Kimberla

I knew I couldn't just walk up to Bailey Hamilton's door at night and knock. I needed to wait and catch the Hamiltons at a weak moment. I figured if she had something to do with Jacob's abduction, then there could even possibly be some in-and-out activity going on around her place.

I drove my rented vehicle and parked a block from her home. I walked around the back, amazed at how large the property was. I took my time peeping through every window.

Man, I really hoped I wouldn't have to wait too long. It took forever for the hussy to go upstairs so I could get into the house. Finally I looked at my watch about eleven. Around that time Bailey and her husband finally turned off the downstairs lights. I used my locksmithing skills to let myself into the house.

I put my foot on the last step and was happy when I

heard a door close. Hopefully it was their bedroom. I walked up to the door, took out my tranquilizer gun, which looked like the real thing, and flicked on the light. Senator Hamilton was alone.

"Who are you?" he asked in shock. "What do you want?"

I pointed my gun at him and smiled.

"Where's the wife?" I asked in a fake deepened voice.

That question was answered for me. I felt a pistol at the small of my back.

"Put down your gun, you black bastard."

Now I really started to smile. Black bastard? I didn't have to wonder what she thought about black people.

I moved slowly, bending down like I was going to do what she said.

"Don't shoot," I cried, still in a mock deep voice.

"Put it down," Bailey Hamilton insisted.

I sighed. "I would hate to do that. I don't think you know what you're asking me to do."

"Oh, really? I know I would love to blow a hole in your sorry body. Now do as I say. Now!"

From the corner of my eye I saw the senator get off the bed and walk toward me. That's when I made my move.

I swung, chopping Bailey Hamilton clean across the face. She cried out and fell against the door panel. I swung again in the opposite direction and kicked her pistol clean out of her hand, and across the floor. Next I turned to her husband.

I almost laughed. He was cowered on his knees in a praying position. He didn't even try to fight.

"Please," he begged, "please don't hurt us!"

I ignored him. I hated a weak man. Looking around at Bailey Hamilton, I scowled. I hated a racist, too. But at least she was ballsy enough to *try* to fight. Even if she did get her ass kicked.

"Get over there with your pitiful husband," I told her.

With a gun pointing at her swelling face, she had no choice but to follow my directions.

"What do you want from us?" Bailey asked. "Money? It has to be money. That's how your type is. You don't work for anything. You just attack poor innocent people and take!"

"Shut the hell up, woman! I don't want your money. I want answers. Where is Jacob White?"

The senator looked at his wife nervously but curiously. Perhaps he didn't know what was going on; perhaps he was innocent. But either way, he was guilty by association. She for sure knew exactly what I was talking about.

"I don't know," she started to say.

"Don't even try it. I know all about you and your despicable brother. Now where is Jacob White?" I cocked my gun. That seemed to not even faze the woman. She still didn't blink. But her husband—

"He's at our vacation home about forty miles away, 5311 Shelia Road."

For some reason I didn't trust that. "Why would you have a vacation house in Boston? Nobody vacations in their home city."

The senator nodded rapidly. "We rent it out. It's just an investment. I swear I'm telling you the truth!"

If looks could kill he'd be one dead fool. Bailey's eyes were shooting daggers at her husband.

"Shut up!" she told him.

"No, you shut up. I'm tired of all these sick games you and your brothers are playing. And look at us now."

"Brothers? You mean brother, don't you?" I asked.

"No. Miles got your Jacob White. I promise you, everything I'm saying is the gospel truth." The senator looked at me as if pleading. "Please don't kill me."

I had to trust what he was telling me. I honestly didn't have a choice.

"Okay," I said. "Now I'm really sorry I have to do this."

"Do what?" he asked. He screamed "no" when he saw where my gun was headed.

I aimed first at Bailey, and pulled the trigger. Her husband screamed, then looked at me, knowing he was next.

"Please don't...don't..."

I pointed at him and fired again. Within seconds, they were both unconscious.

"That should keep you two quiet for a while."

I turned and rushed out of the room and down the stairs.

"Don't worry, Jacob. Don't worry, baby," I said out loud, as if he could hear me.

"I'm coming. Just hold on. I'm coming."

I prayed I wasn't too late.

CHAPTER 23

Jacob

Have you ever felt so tired, so drained both mentally and physically, that you couldn't close your eyes?

My pain had caused spikes to grow under my eyelids. It was as if I had them holding my eyes open, forbidding me to sleep.

Miles had the decency to remove Anthony's body. But I still couldn't get the image of what had happened to him out of my mind.

It was all my fault. I should have let him come to Boston alone. Or better yet, I shouldn't have gotten him involved at all. Now I would have the daunting task of explaining to his wife and kids why he was not coming home to them. The way things were going, I probably wouldn't be alive to explain anything. That thought gave me an electric shock. I didn't want to die. I had too much left to do in my life. I had to find a way to get my lady back. And I was not going to allow Bree to have to mourn another parent leaving her.

I was starting to get chills. The house was cool, and lack

of water, pissy pants, and an all-over dehydrated feeling had for sure changed my body temperature.

The door cracked. I sat up abruptly. I figured it was Miles coming to taunt me some more, shoot me like he did Anthony, or maybe put another cigarette out on my face.

He was taking a while to get in, and he obviously wasn't using a key. I couldn't help but wonder why.

The door swung open and the lights came on. It wasn't Miles. It was a small-framed boy who oddly enough, reminded me of...

"Kimberla?"

"Shh," she whispered. "Are you here alone?"

"Hell yeah, I am! Hurry up and untie me. How did you find me?"

Kimberla had already moved behind me to loosen my hands. She stopped and grabbed my chin so that my eyes met hers.

"Did you doubt for one minute that I wouldn't find you, Jacob?"

Her eyes were tender and filled with unabashed love. It shocked me with its intensity. Whenever we had talked about feelings, or love, Kimberla always turned it into a cutesy joke. There was no joke in her eyes now. It was real.

"I'm just so glad you're here," I said.

She smiled. "I'm parked just down the road. We have to hurry."

I wanted to hug her, kiss her. But I knew she was right. Miles could be coming around any time.

Once I was loose I got up and pulled Kimberla into my arms.

"Did you come here alone?" I asked.

"Yes," she said, hugging me back. "But I already alerted Kyte and the local FBI and police. They should be here soon."

She smiled sweetly at me, and then touched the burn mark on my cheek. She smiled in concern. "Let's go."

The sound of someone pulling up in the driveway made us both pause.

"I want you to hide," I told her. "Give me your gun."

"But, Jacob—"

"Just give me your gun!" I whispered anxiously.

Once she had handed it to me, I closed it in my hand, sat down in the chair, and put my hands behind my back. Kimberla had hidden behind the sofa. The door opened. It was Miles.

"Well," he said. "Still no word from your people. I guess they don't care about you." He smirked.

He suddenly looked around me. I noticed Kimberla had gotten up from behind the sofa, damn her, and started walking toward Miles.

"Who the hell are you?" he said.

He reached behind him as if to grab his gun. It all happened in slow motion. I pointed my gun to his upper body, and pulled the trigger. Once, in the chest. Miles looked down, confused. He seemed surprised that he wasn't invincible. He looked up at me and Kimberla and tried to raise his gun. I pulled the trigger again, this time landing one right between his eyes.

The room was quiet after that, but smelled of gun powder. Kimberla walked over and hugged me again.

"I told you to stay back."

"I know," she said. "I just didn't want to give him too much momentum. Besides, I could have easily kicked that ass."

"Yeah, I know you could have." I laughed at her.

We quietly watched his body lying there for a moment.

Police sirens roared. We both felt relief that we were no longer alone. I felt as if I had been let out of a trap. It seemed as if I had been stuck in this house for days. Kimberla pulled off her facial disguise. I was glad about that. I'd much rather see her pretty face.

"Do you know where he took Anthony?" she asked.

"No. I'm hoping Bailey Hamilton knows. That's Miles and Malcolm's sister."

She nodded. "Yes, I know the whole story. She and her husband should be..." She looked at her watch. "They should be waking up about now. In handcuffs."

"Don't tell me you did the old tranquilizer thing with them?"

"Sure did." Kimberla grinned. "And you should have seen the senator's face when he thought I had killed his sourpuss wifey. It was a trip! But you know, we have a lot to talk about, Jacob. The worst part of this is that Malcolm is still out there. And he is coming after both of us."

I looked Kimberla up and down. "Are you scared?"

"Negro, please!" She rolled her eyes.

I couldn't help but laugh. Fear was not in my baby's MO.

"Let's go home," she said.

I put my arms around her shoulders, and we walked out the door, together.

Catwomyn75

The music was mellow and R&B chill. She wasn't feeling very mellow, though. She felt pissed.

Alonzo had agreed to meet, but he wasn't playing by the rules. She couldn't deal with those types. Why couldn't he just play by the fucking rules!

"I'm bored," she said. "I thought you wanted to be alone."

"Baby, we are alone. Ain't nobody in this room but us."

"What about your friend over there?"

He must have thought she was some kind of trick. How dare he set up a meeting with her and then tell her later he had a friend joining them? He wanted some sick three-some, and that wasn't her way. That put her in a situation. She couldn't handle two at a time. She had to figure something out.

Leroy, Alonzo's so-called friend, was puffing on a joint. He got up, walked over to her, and felt her ass. She jerked back.

"Damn, sorry, Ma," he said. His eyes stayed on her as he spoke to his friend. "Zo, I thought you said she was down for this."

Alonzo looked at her inquiringly. "You are, aren't you, Jami?"

Jami smiled and looked at both of them seductively.

"Sure I am. But I'm thirsty. Why don't you two boys go get us some wine? I'll take a quick shower, wash all my cracks and crevices, and when you get back..." She moaned. "Mmmmm...we can have some adult fun."

"Whoa!" they both said in unison.

She wanted to lock them both out the door. This was the bad thing about meeting men online. Sometimes you got hooked up with the kooks and psychos.

Alonzo got up and grabbed his keys.

Leroy nudged his arm.

"Yo, Zo, what if she ain't here when we get back, man?"

They both looked at the woman they called Jami.

She shrugged her shoulders and opened her blouse. "Where am I supposed to be going?"

She ran her finger up and down between her breasts.

"Yeah," he said. "Yeah, she wants it. She ain't going nowhere."

He and Leroy smiled at each other as they walked out the hotel door.

Once they were gone, she got up and looked in the mirror. She grabbed her purse, took out her lipstick, and refreshed it. The charm bracelet her dead husband had given her jingled on her arm.

"Freaking high-ass, dogs," she said out loud.

She put her lipstick back in her bag and walked out the door. Once she was driving down the street, she checked her cell phone.

"Shit!" she said, banging her steering wheel in frustration.

Another need came over her. She felt this need almost like one would need air to breathe. Maybe she had struck out with Alonzo, but she had a long list of male dogs she could toss a bone to.

Once she got home, she would get on her computer, and do just that.

CHAPTER 24

Kimberla

There was hell to pay once we got back to Maryland. Of course Kyte was livid that I had gone out on my own to find and rescue Jacob. He knew me well enough not to be surprised, though.

He had both Jacob and me placed on round-the-clock police protection until they could locate Malcolm, or so Kyte claimed. That was the worst thing he could do to me. I am the type of person who likes to fight her own battles. The Malcolm thing was a complete mystery. Nobody could just disappear off the face of the earth, the way Malcolm did, without someone helping him. Actually he had before, but that's what worried Jacob and me.

I felt kind of bad. I loved my job, but I was quickly losing faith.

Jacob was at Holy Cross Hospital getting IV fluids until he got some of his strength back. I felt weird when I saw police officers standing outside his door.

"Oh, there you are," I said sarcastically. "Has anyone come to chop up Jacob yet?"

"Funny, ha, ha," Ives Franklin said.

I knew Ives from him having been with the bureau for a while. It was funny that now they would have him protecting Jacob. He was a real cool guy.

I walked past him and his partner, gave him a shove with my elbow, and opened Jacob's room door.

"Keep playing," Ives shouted. "I'll be guarding you next, Chameleon!"

I ignored that.

"Hey!" I exclaimed once I was in the room. I walked over to Jacob's bed and pulled up a chair. "How are you feeling?"

"I feel fine. I don't really need to be here. Keep trying to tell these damn doctors that."

He did look better. His face looked slightly lean and ragged, but on the whole he looked pretty good. Considering he had gone two days without food or water.

"They're just being careful. I agree that you're safer in here than out on the streets."

"Oh?" He looked at me closely. "And what about you?"

"Like Ives just said, I'm Chameleon. I'm a bad-ass chick."

"Right!"

I snorted. "You bet I'm right. Man, I can't even take a hot piss without being followed or asked where I'm going and if I'm okay."

We laughed together. Jacob paused, and looked at me seriously.

"I really miss you, Kimmy. I hope once all this is over we can have a fresh start."

"I miss you, too. Jacob, I don't know…"

"What don't you know? I know you love me."

Of course I loved him. I was scared. There were so many things, so many fears and dreams that I hadn't shared with him. It was about time I did.

"I just have a lot I need to tell you," I said.

The door creaked open. We both looked up to see who it was.

"Coming in," a voice called out. It was Lolita. "Hey," she said. "How are you two doing?"

"I'm fine," I answered. I looked at Jacob, waiting for him to answer for himself.

"I'm doing fine," he said. "But I'll be much better once I'm out of here."

"I can imagine."

Lolita looked at both of us. She seemed a little uncomfortable. I guess she thought I was going to trip because she had come to visit Jacob. I guess I had been giving the poor chickadee a hard time. Actually, after everything Jacob and I had gone through, I didn't even care about stuff like that anymore. Nearly losing someone you love has a way of making you appreciate them so much more.

"Kimberla, can I talk to you for a minute?" Lolita asked.

"Sure."

She seemed a little weird. Maybe this wasn't about the jealousy thing with her and me over Jacob.

I leaned over and gave Jacob a kiss on the tip of his nose. "I'll be right back."

Lolita and I walked past Ives. He smiled when I made a fist at him.

"Yeah, hit me, girl. I love ballsy women!"

"Shut up," I told him.

Lolita laughed. "What's up with him?"

"He's just crazy," I responded.

We took the elevator down to the main floor. I wanted to get some air, so we decided to talk outside in the garden area of the hospital.

"So what's up?"

Lolita didn't answer. I stretched a little and yawned in my chair. I was feeling so tired. When I opened my eyes, she was again looking at me strangely.

"What the hell is wrong with you?" I asked.

"You know I've been working on the Soroco case alone while you were gone, right?"

"Oh yes, I know. I'm so sorry, Lolita. I know I haven't been the best on this case. There's just been so much going on." I frowned.

I really had lost interest. I had totally forgotten about anything but saving Jacob. Maybe this was a little birdie in my ear, telling me it was time for me to move on.

"Have you learned anything new about Bianca Greenwich?"

"No." Lolita nodded. "But I did learn some interesting things about your friend Kendra Gray."

"What?" I shouted and stood up. "Lolita, what is your

problem? Why are you insisting on pinning this madness on Kendra?"

I walked over to the window. I couldn't handle this. I didn't understand Lolita's persistence. Did she really hate me so much that she wanted to discredit my friend?

"Do you know how her husband died, Kimberla?"

I swung around. "I should. She's one of my best friends."

"He died the same way all the murder victims died. Do you know her husband was bisexual? Do you know that she had an aunt in Thurmont?"

"I don't want to hear any more! I don't want to hear no more of your bullshit! I'm out of here, Lolita."

"No, wait." She stood in front of me, blocking my entrance.

"I don't have anything else to say to you. If you're mad because you want Jacob, that's one thing. But taking it to the degree of trying to destroy someone I love is just ridiculous. I'm going back inside!"

The squealing wheels of a dark sedan with tinted windows pulling up grabbed our attention. When the driver window rolled down and I saw the flash of black metal, I fell to the ground. I grabbed Lolita by the arm to pull her down with me as the sounds of gunfire ripped through the air. I pressed my body against the ground and closed my eyes. When I opened them again, Lolita was lying facedown on the ground.

"No!" I screamed. "No!"

* * *

It was all too much, all the accusations, all the events that led up to now. Lolita was hanging on for dear life in the hospital, and they said she would pull through, but still it was just too much. I was at home with Jacob and Kyte. Kyte was questioning me privately about what had happened with the attack on me and Lolita. I felt so bad because I didn't dare tell him what Lolita had said to me. How could I tell anyone?

"You two are to stay right here," Kyte demanded. "This has gotten crazy. Malcolm is a madman."

"Oh, come on, Kyte. Don't act like you didn't know he was crazy. That's what I don't get about this whole jacked-up case. What are you hiding? What does Malcolm know that is so important, that it had to come to this?"

"I—I just can't talk about it now. But once we find him, I promise you two will know more."

"Damnit!" Jacob banged his fist against the wall.

I had nothing to say. I sat quietly on the sofa, trying to think of what my next step would be. I hadn't even told Jacob what Lolita had said.

"So now," Jacob was shouting. "Now Anthony is dead, Lolita is hurt, Kimberla and I have a psycho trying to hunt us down, and still you can't say shit?"

Kyte sighed, and then looked down at his watch. "I have to go. You two should be fine here. Just don't leave this suite."

We had been sent to a hotel suite in northeast D.C. Not

that it was bulletproof, but supposedly no one knew about our whereabouts but Kyte, our guards, and us.

"Yeah, go," Jacob said heatedly. "It's not like you're doing us a helluva lot of good."

Kyte look at Jacob and frowned. He walked over to me with his arms stretched out. I got up and gave him a big hug.

"I'll talk to you tomorrow, okay?"

I nodded quietly.

"You two just be careful…"

Once Kyte was out the door, Jacob shouted, "Good riddance!"

He turned around and noticed the look on my face.

"Sorry," he said. "You look stressed."

"No. I'm just worried. Have you checked on Bree?"

Jacob sat down on the couch and reached his arms out. I walked over and cuddled up close to him.

"She's fine. Her grandma lives so far out nobody will ever be able to find her."

"I hope you're right," I said doubtfully.

"Oh, I'm sure of it. Now let's talk about you."

"What about me?"

Jacob's fingers traced my bottom lip. "Let's talk about why you're looking so stressed. What's your mind? I know it's not just about Malcolm, or about what happened to Lolita." He frowned at that. "I know you well enough to know there is something else going on."

"I'm just tired," I said.

Jacob caressed my shoulders. The feel of his touch was slowly relaxing me. I felt the weight of the world lifting.

"Let's go," he whispered.

CHAPTER 25

Jacob

It had been a long time since Kimberla and I had real quality time together. I almost wanted to thank Malcolm for being the hunting jackass that he was.

Kimberla had gone to run a hot bath for us. I was looking for the best jazz channel in Maryland that I could find on the radio. I was usually an R&B man, but I wanted to change up for the night. I finally settled on 106.7 Jazz. The incense was lit. The smell of lavender flowed from the bathroom. I looked in the mirror and didn't feel too upset. The doctors had said my little burn would heal nicely, without too bad of a scar. Everything was perfect.

"I feel kind of bad," Kimberla said from the door.

"Why?" I frowned.

She walked into the bedroom and wrapped her robe tightly around her.

"Everybody we care about is either dead or dying maybe. And here we are, acting like we're on a freaking honeymoon or something."

"Hmm…" I lifted her chin up so that her eyes met mine. "Is that your way of asking me to marry you?"

"Jacob, I'm serious."

So was I, but I didn't want to push my luck too far. *Damn! I really was serious.* I'd think about that revelation later.

"Okay. I know you're serious. Kimberla, you think it doesn't hurt, too, when I think of Anthony? When I think of Lolita? It does, but we can't change it. We can't stop living because of it." I pulled her into my arms. "Tonight is about us. I don't want to think about guilt. I don't want to think about Malcolm or work or any of that bullshit. I just want to think about you, and me. Can we do that? Just for tonight?"

Her eyes answered me. She reached out her hand and we walked slowly into the bathroom.

"You don't have that water boiling hot like you normally do, do you?" I joked.

"No." She smiled. "I remember how sensitive you are."

When we got into the water I pulled her back against me. I knew she could feel my hardness against her backside. Maybe she could understand how much I wanted her, needed her, and how much I missed her being close to me. She leaned her head back and covered my lips with hers. The sweetness of the moment lingered on and on. I rubbed my tongue sensually against hers. We continued making love with our mouths. Sucking and devouring each other. I could feel a rush building in my body, and hers. I pushed her away slightly.

"We'd better get out of this water before it gets cold," I said in a hoarse voice.

"No," she said.

She turned her body around and sat on my lap face forward. She soaped up the washcloth and started rubbing me down with it. I clenched my teeth together when she rubbed and tickled me under my arms.

"Stop," I said, fighting not to laugh.

Kimberla's eyes sparkled. "Okay, Mr. White, stand up."

I stood up, and leaned against the shower wall. Kimberla started washing my lower body. Starting at my ankles she moved upward, to my knees, behind them, up my thighs. When she got in between them, scrubbing at my groin, I braced myself against the wall.

"What's wrong?" she whispered.

I didn't respond. I closed my eyes when she started rubbing softly under my balls. She rubbed from back to front, and then slowly crept up my penis. It jerked against the washcloth. My eyes were still closed but I felt her move away, at least I thought she did.

I was just about to open my eyes when I felt a totally different sensation than the washcloth. She was blowing warm air along my dick. Her eyes were looking up at me and then...

"Ooooo, baby!"

She was licking me with the flat of her tongue. Up and down, then circling the tip, flicking at the pee hole. My body started quivering. It had been so long since she had done this. So damn long!

"Mmm..." she moaned.

I couldn't say anything. All I could do was stand there, or attempt to; stand there and take the delicious assault she was making on my body.

She moved lower, sucking both my testicles into her mouth. As she was sucking, her tongue was licking, lower, teasing the thin line that ran from my balls to my ass. I froze when she did that, and almost stopped her. But the feeling was so incredible I let her have her way.

She pushed against my hips, holding me tight, and then engulfed me. There was no escaping the warmth of her mouth. But then, I didn't want to. She sucked and swirled, groaned and hummed on me. I was gripping the towel racks, almost to the point of yanking them down, but I didn't care.

"Oh," I cried out.

She sucked harder. My knees got weak and I was falling, almost cramping over with the intensity of pleasure. She took me all the way down her throat and held me there. Only her throat muscles were working. I looked down in utter disbelief. I knew I couldn't hold back much longer. Just when I felt the tiny tingles starting to flow from my toes all the way up to where her mouth met me, she pulled off.

I slumped down in the water with a smash. I was about to grab her, try to give her some of the pleasure she had just given me. Before I had a chance to do that, she was in my lap, and I was inside her. The feeling of her hot inner heat was different but just as delicious as her making love to me with her mouth.

She ground and gripped me, rotated her hips around and around. My head was thrown back in abandonment, but I could feel her lips sucking and biting at my neck. Her small breasts were squashed against my chest.

"I love you, Jacob," she moaned out.

I couldn't move, or talk. My mouth was gaping open. My eyes were open, too. I saw the lights above us twirling as my lady made love to me like she never had before. My body jerked in a sudden, strong contraction. We both screamed. I was coming! She was coming! I was shooting inside her, again and again and again. Every heartache, every pain Kimberla and I had gone through for the past few weeks, shot out of my body into hers as if it were a sexual salve.

When it stopped, we both were healed.

Someone was knocking on the door. I opened my eyes, or attempted to, and saw Kyte standing at the bedroom entrance.

"Sorry," he said.

"What are you doing in here?" I almost shouted. That woke Kimberla up. Thankfully she had the covers pulled up on her, so Kyte didn't see anything.

She still screamed and pulled them up closer over her shoulders.

"Kyte, how did you get in here?" she asked.

He gave a light laugh. "I'll give you two a few minutes. I'll be waiting." He laughed again and walked away from the door.

"My God. Can you believe him?"

I could only laugh. My lady looked so cute. Her hair was tossed and she was covered up as if she were shy. After last night she could put that card away.

"I guess that's part of the deal with being public property now," I said.

I ran my fingers alongside her cheek. "Let's get dressed and see what the boss man wants."

Minutes later we were chillin' with Kyte over a cup of coffee.

"Sorry about that," Kyte said. He tried to look embarrassed, but it didn't work. The sucker.

"Hmph! I just bet you are," Kimberla said.

Kyte put his coffee cup down and his expression changed. "Look, on a serious note, I guess it's time I told you two what's going on."

"And I would agree with that," I said. My eyes didn't leave his. This was too long in coming, and two good men had been lost because of secrets.

"Okay." Kyte scratched his head nervously. "We found Malcolm a year ago."

"A year?" I asked. "You have had this monster for a year and you never said anything?"

"Just listen." Kyte put up his hand.

"We knew about Malcolm's dirt before New York, before the Michael Riley case. We didn't know who he was directly involved with. But we needed Malcolm. He promised to turn state's evidence in that drug trade scandal as long as he got a reduction in his own sentence."

"John Hamilton, Bailey Hamilton's husband, is, or was, deeply involved. We needed the information that only Malcolm had."

Kimberla's face had turned dark. I could see anger brimming in her eyes. I rubbed her shoulder to calm her down.

"And Micah is dead, as is Anthony. Lolita is fighting for her life. Jacob almost lost his life and now both of us are prisoners, yet getting some dumb-ass senator was worth all this?" she stormed.

"Kimberla, I'm not saying that. What you don't understand is, John Hamilton is first cousins with—"

"The Vice President," I finished.

Kimberla looked at both of us as if we had lost our minds.

"I don't give a flying fuck who he is first cousins with. A crook is a crook!" she screamed. "Hell, as far as we know, the vice president himself could be a crook, too!"

"He is…"

Kimberla gasped, and I couldn't even close my mouth at that one.

"I know it sounds crazy. But like I told you two, this is bigger and deeper than you could imagine. It's not so simple as let's get Malcolm. It's a possible ongoing corruption, all the way to the White House."

"Wow…" I said quietly. There really was nothing else to say.

Kimberla wasn't as tongue-tied.

"So I guess we are just casualties of war, huh? What about John Hamilton? He knew about Miles abducting Jacob and Anthony. He knew everything his wife knew."

"At this point we can't pin anything legally wrong on her, Kimberla. It's all resting on Malcolm Johnson's testimony. That's why it's so important that we find him. Alive!"

Kyte got up and walked to the door. What he just told us explained things a little more. But it sure didn't make Kimberla or me feel any better. We were pawns in a political game of chess. All we could do was sit back and hope we were crowned before we got jumped.

"Oh!" Kyte turned and handed Kimberla a folder. "I saw Lolita last night. I explained to her why you haven't called, so she understands. She told me to give you this."

Kimberla looked at the folder, and frowned.

CHAPTER 26

Kimberla

I paced back and forth with my arms wrapped tightly around me. We were all a game to them. It killed me that the bureau honestly had so little regard for its agents they would let all this happen, just for the sake of nabbing that pitiful Senator Hamilton. And his even more pitiful vice president cousin. Micah was worth ten of them. And he was gone.

"You plan to walk a hole in the floor?" Jacob asked with sarcastic humor.

"What? Jacob, aren't you angry?"

"Of course I am, but what good will it do right now, babe? We just have to chill and let things run their course. At this point there's nothing we can do. You know that."

"But I don't have to like it!"

"No, you don't," Jacob said softly. "But we are having our make-believe honeymoon, remember? I wish I could make you feel better all the time."

My mood instantly softened. Jacob looked so relaxed

and beautiful sitting there. He was right. There was no need, at this point, trippin' about something neither of us could change.

I smiled and went to join him on our purple couch. I flopped down beside him.

"You know, this couch is really ugly!" I said.

"No, it's not. I was thinking about asking if I could have it. I mean, it's the least they could do."

He had to be joking. And my face told him so.

"You're beautiful," he said, kissing me.

I blushed. "No, I'm not. I'm passable."

"You're beautiful to me."

We both were quiet. I was thinking about the beautiful comment. I next learned that Jacob was thinking about something else he once said...

"Kimmy, you said we had to talk. I had hoped you were ready to tell me what you've been hiding from me. Please don't say it's nothing."

I froze. "What—"

"That look. It's the same look that comes on your face whenever I try to really *know* you."

He took my hands in his and kissed my palms.

"You do love me, right? Do you trust me?" he asked.

"Yes, I do, very much."

I was shaking. I knew I had to talk to him. I knew it was now or never. I closed my eyes and let all my nightmares spill out.

* * *

*I was seventeen, and had the biggest crush on this bas-
ketball player named Chris Brown. I was never one of the
pretty girls. So I never thought I had a chance with
someone like him, just from the physical standpoint. But
I was smart, and sassy. Chris seemed to like that.*

*We played flirt games together. Of course he never did
it around anyone who would notice. But I didn't care. I
liked him so much.*

*One day after school, I'll never forget it. I rushed home.
I had a dance recital the next night. It was my first solo
and I wanted it to be perfect. I was dancing to a jazzy
version of Peggy Lee's "Fever." I used to live that song.
Now I hate it to this day.*

*I changed into a sports bra and shorts, and had just put
on my music when the telephone rang.*

"Hello?" I said.

"Kimberla. Hey, baby girl?"

*"Hi, Chris," I said. I was blushing so hard. I looked in
the decorative mirror that was in our living room. My face
looked hot!*

"What you doing?"

"Just, um…practicing my dance," I stammered out.

"I bet you got some hot moves."

*I didn't say anything. I didn't dare! Was Chris calling
me hot?*

"Well?"

"What?" I felt and sounded dumb, I knew. I hadn't heard a word he had said.

Chris laughed at me. "I said why don't you let me come over and check it out? Is your mom home?"

"No, she's not. But I don't know if she would like that. I'm not really supposed to let anyone in."

I was biting my bottom lip. I felt so excited that Chris actually wanted to come see me. On the other hand, I knew my mom. If she came home and found a boy in the house, I wouldn't be dancing to "Fever." I'd have a fever from her going upside my head.

"Oh, okay. It's no big deal. Your girl Kendra home? My boy Freddy wanted to talk to her. I wanna do something. I guess we could go over there," Chris said. He sounded kind of mad.

I started panicking. Kendra was my best friend. But I'd be damned if I wanted a boy I liked to call her or go see her. I looked at the clock. It would be about an hour and a half before my mom got home from work.

"I think Kendra has cheerleading practice today," I lied. I knew she was home. "Maybe, well, maybe you could come over for a little while. But my mom gets home at five-thirty."

Chris's voice cheered up right away. Dang, I thought. He really did like me!

"Well, open the door, baby girl."

"What do you mean open the door?"

"I'm at Jamal's house, across the street. I'm hanging up now."

I giggled. But he was gone. I was so excited. *Oh my god!* I thought. *I didn't have time to brush my teeth or anything. What if he wanted to kiss me?*

I was about to run upstairs and see if I could spare the time, but before one foot touched the first step, the doorbell rang. I ran to the door and opened it without looking out the peephole.

It wasn't just Chris. It was him and Jamal from across the street, and another boy that I didn't recognize. I looked at Chris, feeling very confused.

"Hey," he said. "I hope you don't mind. My boys wanted to see you move, too. You know Jamal, and this is James." He nodded toward the other guy. Jamal closed the door, locked it, and looked at me, smiling.

I didn't like this. I looked at Chris and shook my head. "Chris, I thought it was just you coming over."

"Oh," he said, laughing kind of weird. "You don't want my boys over?"

A little alarm went off in my head. I didn't know if I was being silly or not. It just didn't feel right.

"No, I don't," I said quietly. "I guess you should call me another time."

I went to open the door so the guys would leave, but James grabbed me from behind.

"But we want to see you right now," he said in a husky voice.

He pulled me tight against him. When Jamal came and stood in front of me, I really knew something was wrong. Something bad was going to happen. He put his hands on my sports bra and squeezed my breasts. I reached up and slapped him. I somehow got away, and started running upstairs. I could hear the guys coming up the stairs behind me. It was weird, all I could think about was that my momma was gonna kill me.

I was able to reach my bedroom. I figured I would get in and lock the door. I had a phone in there and would be able to call someone, maybe Kendra! I heard someone turn the music up. So that gave me a false sense of security, thinking they hadn't followed me right away. I was wrong.

Someone grabbed me by the neck, and pushed my face into my bedroom door. It busted my lip and I could taste my own blood. I screamed.

"Oh! Don't!" I cried. "Please, leave!"

I somehow ended up on the floor. I saw James and Jamal. Jamal had his foot on my chest, pushing down on me. James was standing beside him. I looked toward the door and Chris was walking through it, unbuckling his pants. All of them were laughing.

"I get her first," Chris said. "I thought you were gonna show me those moves, baby girl?"

He was down, leaning over me. I felt him rip my shorts off. When I tried to push him off, I couldn't. James and Jamal were each holding one of my arms. All I could do was lie there and beg, and cry.

"Chris, don't do this! Please, stop!"

I screamed even louder once he was on top of me. And pain filled my body.

Jacob was quiet for a long time after I told him my story. He just held me. He knew exactly what I needed. But oddly enough, after telling him, I wasn't afraid anymore. I knew I had just eradicated my demons.

"Did they ever get caught?"

"No. I cleaned myself up. I told my mom I had tripped and busted my lip. I went through the rest of the school year with Chris and Jamal laughing at me whenever I walked down the hallway."

"Kimberla, why have you never told me this? Why did you keep it inside so long?"

"What was I supposed to say?" I cried. "Everyone has always looked at me like I'm this strong person. I wanted people to see that. That's how I survived. It's how I dealt with that nightmare."

I looked at him, begging for understanding. "When I started loving you, it was hard to admit it. I always felt that love meant weakness. Like the weakness I had for Chris. It was easy to push other men away. But you were different. You wouldn't accept anything else. I had gotten to the point that I was willing to lose you rather than let you know a side of me that wasn't always the Chameleon, the kick-ass girl. I had to be strong, Jacob. Can't you see?"

My eyes were overflowing with tears. I always knew

that if I ever really let them start, they would never stop. But somehow it felt different. It was as if a sore scab was lifting off the huge cut that rested over my heart.

Jacob held my face between both of his big hands. He was kissing my tears. It was like a soothing that God had sent.

"You are strong, baby. And you don't need to be hard in order to show you're strong." He pulled back and looked deeply at me. "Right now I'm looking at the strongest, the sexiest, sweetest Chameleon in the world. And I love her like a hot plate of chitterlings."

I laughed. "You are so silly. Leave it to you to mention chitterlings. Them funky things!"

"Naw, girl. They are good. I'm gonna feed you them sometime. I always tell you that."

"Right!"

My nose was swollen but I felt so good. I felt loved and free for the first time in my adult life. It was all due to Jacob. It was funny how I could talk about the worst experience of my life, something that had plagued me forever, and then be able to laugh moments later.

"Thank you, Jacob," I whispered.

"For what?"

I shook my head. There was no more need for words. "Just thanks. Go take your shower, okay? I'm gonna look over Lolita's folder."

"All right." He looked back at me when he reached the bedroom door. "You sure you don't want to join me? I love your water games. Wink, wink." He winked as he said the words.

"Get out of here," I said, laughing.

All laughter ended once he was gone and I opened the folder. When I had finished reading it, the unfamiliarity of tears was mine again.

CHAPTER 27

Kimberla

I raced down to get to Kendra's apartment. I knew it wouldn't be long before Jacob discovered I was gone. I just needed to talk to her. I needed her to tell me from her own mouth that it wasn't true.

Memories flashed before my eyes. Her and me as little girls, playing in the park; her and me at our high school graduation, excited and happy about our futures and college. The person I grew up with, the person I stood up for at her wedding when she was marrying the man of her dreams, could not be this same person. It could not be this Catwomyn75 who had been viciously murdering men for months.

"It's not true," I said to myself.

I pulled up at her condo and switched off my engine. I took a deep breath, got out of the car, and made my way to her door.

I was going to knock, but decided instead to let myself in. Kendra and I had always kept keys to each other's apartments. Just for safety reasons.

When I opened the door, I was confronted with the same clean, well-kept home that was a staple for Kendra. I walked inside and closed the door. Pictures of her and me graced one side of the living room wall. African pictures, which I had given her, dressed the other.

For some reason, seeing these things gave me comfort. I felt somehow the familiarity of her place proved that my friend was the same woman I had always known. She couldn't be the person Lolita said she was. She couldn't be the person described in the folder, full of evidence pointing against her.

I sat on the couch and covered my face with my hands. When I removed them, I spotted her computer. The monitor was clear in view from where I sat. I got up to check it out.

Jacob

I couldn't even talk for the screaming and shouting Kyte polluted my ear with.

"Where is she? How could she just disappear from the hotel and you not know where she is?"

"Kyte, calm down!"

I paced the floor back and forth. I felt just as bad as Kyte did. I couldn't even tell him that the reason she was able to dip out as quickly as she did was that she had me so zonked out by all that good lovin'. I had just taken a quick shower. My mind was filled with everything she had told me about her childhood, about her rape. It made so much sense now. The need she felt to be so tough; how hard she fought against allowing any man to get close to her.

After we made love, I was so dazed at how good it was. I was in awe that she had opened up to me, finally. She loved me, she really loved me. Now she was gone!

"Has she tried to call you?" Kyte asked me.

"No. If she had you know I would have told you."

"As soon as she does you call me ASAP! This has gotten insane. I cannot have agents popping up dead all over the place. And I don't want to lose Kimberla."

"Neither do I, Kyte," I said somberly. "Neither do I."

Kimberla

One after another, pictures of men popped up on Kendra's computer. I flipped through e-mail after e-mail. All had the user names of the murdered men, addressed to my best friend and her Internet name, Catwomyn75.

I felt like I was suffocating. I couldn't deny what was before my eyes if I wanted to.

"Why, Kendra?" I said aloud.

Why couldn't she come to me if she was hurting this badly? I thought about all the long talks we'd had. She was always the strong one, always telling me how to handle hurt and pain and disappointment. I was too self-ishly thinking about myself and the bogus issues I thought I had with Jacob that I couldn't see my friend needed me.

My cell phone buzzed again. I sighed and looked at it.

Jacob had called about four times. There was no need to hide any of this from him or anyone else now. I also had to find Kendra.

"Jacob."

"Kimmy, where are you? Why did you leave like that?"

"I'm at Kendra's place."

"Stay there!"

"No, listen. It's Kendra. It's been Kendra all along." I choked on my words.

"What are you talking about, baby? What do you mean it's Kendra?"

"The Soroco murders. I read Lolita's files. It was all there. But I didn't want to believe it. I'm at Kendra's place now and it's all true."

"Okay." Jacob's voice was calm. "I want you to just wait for me. I'll be there in fifteen minutes."

"I will."

"Promise me, Kimberla!"

"I'm not going anywhere, Jacob."

After he hung up, I clicked on more e-mails. These were more recent.

There was one that really caught my attention. It was dated with today's date:

Meet me at the motel in Catonsville. If you want some of these goodies. *smile*

What the hell! My heart started beating faster. I clicked on the next e-mail she had sent.

See you in the morning. Eleven is good. Mmm... I can't wait to taste you. Buh-bye!

I didn't need to read any more. I didn't have any time to call anyone. I needed to get to Catonsville, before it was too late!

The traffic seemed to be dragging, and irritating the hell out of me. There was a gasoline rig that decided today was a good day to break down in the middle of the interstate. I subconsciously patted my hands on the steering wheel, as if that would make the rig get the hell out of the way.

I was horrified. So many things were going through my mind. A thought of Lolita flashed before me, and what had happened to her. I may not have liked her, but I respected her as an agent. She had been what I always prized in myself, until now that is. She was an agent who didn't allow personal issues to get in the way of her job, and who pressed on to the finish.

My mind flicked back to Kendra. I shook my head in disbelief. Some things she had said echoed in my ears. The antimale views she had sometimes. The fact that she hadn't dated since her husband died. The periods of time she would disappear without any word. Not that any of that would automatically point to her as a serial killer.

It was so weird. All the evidence that Lolita had gathered pointed directly to Kendra, yet part of me still remembered the kind, gentle soul I had grown up with. This was the same girl who cried if someone was mean to a kitten. The same person who couldn't stand to see another human being in pain. This love for life was what made Kendra want to be a doctor. It didn't fit. It didn't make sense. It was hard to equate that same person with the one who could so viciously kill three men she didn't even know.

Minutes later the traffic slowly began to speed up to a normal pace. I found myself making headway to the Catonsville motel. Deep inside I was hoping I was wrong; that she wouldn't be there. But fifteen minutes later, I spotted the dark-blue Jeep that for sure was the described vehicle of the murderer. Kendra. I got out of my car and rushed to the office of the hotel. A short Asian man greeted me.

"You need room?" he asked.

"No." I showed him my FBI badge. "I'm looking for anyone who has registered at your hotel within the past hour. It's very important. A female, around thirty years old, but looks younger. Thin, pretty black woman?"

"Sorry. No black woman signed in today."

Ugh. I was getting frustrated at his lack of concern. And the stench of tobacco in the room didn't help, either. I had to hold my nose to breathe.

"Okay, what about a black male, then?" I pressed.

"I'm not sure."

"Well, find out, damnit! Look on your computer. Just give me all registered guests for the last two hours. I also need a master key."

My cell phone rang. I ignored the stupefied look on the attendant's face and answered.

"Kimberla, I'm at Kendra's apartment. Why did you leave? Woman, you're trying to make me crazy!" Jacob shouted.

"Jacob, I couldn't stay. She has plans to do it again. I found it on her computer after I talked to you!"

"Okay, calm down, babe. I'm sorry I screamed at you. Where are you right now?"

"I'm at a motel in Catonsville."

I grabbed the key and registration printouts from the attendant. There were two men who had registered in the past hour. One was a sixty-three-year-old man, according to his license information. The other was a twenty-nine-year-old by the name of Lamone Williams. Sounded black enough for me, and a perfect match, agewise, to her other victims. Bingo.

"Kimmy, are you there?"

"I gotta go, Jacob. I'll call you back."

"No. Listen—"

I clicked off my cell. I knew I didn't have any time to waste.

CHAPTER 28

Kimberla

Minutes seemed to turn into hours. The faster I ran to Lamone Williams's room, the longer it felt that it took to get there. I was finally sliding the key card through the slot. The light didn't blink green, it blinked yellow. *Ugh,* I thought.

"Kendra! Kendra, are you in there?"

I tried the door again. This time, thank God, it turned green. I pushed the door open, hard. There was music playing. The room was dark, so I flicked on the light. I could make out a body, lying on the bed; a man's body.

"Oh, Kendra…" I said sadly.

I was too late. I was too late to save Lamone Williams, and too late to save Kendra from what she had become.

"Hey, girlfriend."

I looked toward the voice. Kendra was sitting at the guest table. She was smiling at me as if there wasn't a body lying in front of us. I didn't even have to check. I knew he was dead.

"Kendra, why?" I walked over to her and got down on

my knees in front of her. Her eyes were glazed as if she weren't really there.

"Why?" I asked her again.

"Why?" Kendra looked at me as if she couldn't understand my question. She pointed to the body that used to be Lamone Williams. "He was one of them, Kimberla. He was the enemy."

"What are you talking about?" I grabbed Kendra by the shoulders. "What are you talking about, girl? What did that man ever do to you? What did any of them ever do to you?"

"They were like Demetrius," Kendra whispered. "I was saving us from them. They were all like him."

"Kendra..."

"Liars, cheats. Down low, homos. Not caring who they hurt—not caring who they lied to, infected because of their sick lifestyles." She looked at me as if I should understand. "I'm a shero," she said, laughing. "I'm a shero, girl! I'm like Robin Hood."

"You killed—" My voice cracked on my words. "You killed Demetrius because he was gay?"

"Ohhhhh, Kimmy," Kendra said in almost a catlike moan of pain. Her shoulders shook violently. "He hurt me so b-b-b-bad! I loved him so much. But I wasn't enough. You see, you see?" She looked up at me; I cried with her.

"I could have dealt with it if it was another woman. That's normal. But a man? They don't know what they do to us. They don't know how it makes a woman feel.

She loses her womanhood. It makes you feel so worthless, so ugly. You give your life to someone, your world. And they just rip it to shreds!"

I covered my mouth with my hands. I could feel her pain, but I couldn't even imagine the depth of it. It was like her dam had broken.

"Who could I tell?" she whispered. "Who could I tell and they not think it was me? It was something missing inside me that my man preferred a man over me. What kind of woman does that make me? I had to stop the pain. But it wouldn't stop, even after Demetrius stopped breathing. It wouldn't stop!"

She looked over at her victim's body. The look in her eyes changed to one of hatred. "I didn't kill anyone who was innocent. He was a sick pervert. Creeping in his sick chat rooms. His sick message boards looking for dick, and then faking with women, pretending like his ass wasn't gay. He deserved it. I wish I could kill him again. Every fucking one of them! Every fucking one of them deserved it!"

My friend was gone. I could hear it in her every word. She believed and she meant every word she said. She honestly didn't see anything wrong with what she had done. I pulled her into my arms and let her cry.

"How touching," a voice mocked from the doorway. It was Malcolm Johnson, clapping as if he had just witnessed a circus performance. "Well," he said, "aren't you going to arrest her, Kimberla Bacon?"

"Malcolm." My voice was bland. "How did you find me?"

He laughed. "My dear Chameleon. I always knew where you were. Who the hell do you think you're dealing with? Do you honestly think you ever got over on me? You're a damn fake and flop and you always have been. Nobody could see through you but me."

I moved away from Kendra. I was struggling in my mind, trying to think of what to do. I knew Malcolm was a madman. I walked over to the bed where Lamone Williams lay.

"So are you going to kill me now?" I looked at Malcolm holding a gun and laughed. "That's what this is all about, isn't it? Your vengeance?"

"I could have killed you anytime. It was my game, not yours."

"Right," I said, and my head flew back in laughter. "That's what your dead brother said before he gave up the ghost."

Malcolm's eyes turned dark. I figured he was going to fire at me, and I really didn't care. I was tired of running from him. I was tired of all the people he had hurt, just to get to me.

He pointed his gun, and he did fire, but not at me. I screamed as Kendra fell to the floor.

"Kendra!"

Malcolm was laughing. He was laughing! I saw red. I saw Micah lying in a pool of blood, because of Malcolm.

I saw Jacob, bent over in that chair, in pain and distraught, because of Malcolm. I saw Lolita, lying on the ground, barely alive, because of Malcolm. His laughter gave me the strength I needed.

Before he could fire another round, this time at me, my foot was off the floor and kissing his face. His nose splattered with blood and jiggled on his face. I knew it was broken. That almost made me laugh. He was a coward, as he always was. He was fine as long as he had his gun or his flunkies to battle for him. But he knew he was now going to have to go hand-to-hand with me. Malcolm knew who was going to win this battle.

I kicked him again, and again. He fell against the wall. I remembered all my training that I had been teaching others for years. The spirit of my art. To the side of his face, to his windpipe, his ribs. He moaned in pain.

When I finished he didn't move. I wanted to keep on, but in my blurred vision I saw Kendra. I fell to the floor and pulled her into my arms.

"Oh, Kendra," I cried. "I'm sorry, sorry, I'm so sorry for what he did to you!"

I held her and cried. Her blood soaked my blouse. I just held her, and rocked and rocked. I didn't hear Malcolm get up. I was too distraught. I was tired. But I felt the cold pistol aimed at the back of my head.

"You bitch!" he snarled through broken teeth. "I am so sick of you!"

I closed my eyes and waited for him to fire.

I heard three shots go off, but I wasn't feeling any pain. I opened my eyes and saw Jacob standing at the door with the hotel manager hiding behind him.

"Jacob!" I ran to him.

"You're safe, baby," he said. He grabbed me into his arms. "It's gonna be all right."

EPILOGUE

Kimberla

I felt so secure in Jacob's arms. It was as if every bad thought, every bad dream, all the walls that held me prisoner, without me even knowing it, had come tumbling down. I breathed a deep sigh of relief and held on tight as he stroked my back.

"How do you feel right now?" Jacob asked me.

"Happy, safe, secure. I dunno…"

I looked up at him and saw his smile, bright as sunrise. His eyes were glazed, coated with content and love. For once, I knew what it was like to totally trust someone, with no reservations. I reached up and caressed his cheek.

"Kyte's not very happy with us."

I nodded in agreement. Kyte hadn't been very happy at all that his pet witness was dead, and so were his chances of nailing the vice president. I didn't even feel bad. There was so much corruption at the top, where would it ever stop anyhow? He also wasn't very happy when both Jacob and I had given him our badges. He was shocked, actually.

"Do you regret quitting?" Jacob asked me.

"No, do you?"

"Hell no! I got the best partner a man could have. I can't wait to start Bacon 'n White Investigators with you."

I bent my head to the side. "You like that name?" I asked.

"I love it. Even though, White-on-White PIs sounds a bit better."

"Hmm..." I scratched my chin. "But my last name is not White."

"Yet!"

I looked down at the huge diamond ring glittering on my left hand. "I can't wait..."

Jacob squeezed my shoulder.

"Kimmy, I'm so sorry about Kendra. I know it has to be hard for you," he said with regret.

I smiled sadly. "I don't have much luck with friends, do I? You know what bothers me the most? She was so unhappy. She was so disturbed, and I was too wrapped up in my own feelings, I didn't even notice it. When her husband died, I knew it was something weird and unnatural. Her reaction to it, you know? But I didn't read her, and with us being friends for so long, I should have been there for her. It should never have come to this..."

Jacob pulled the silken covers more securely over us. I started relaxing again, knowing he understood exactly what I was feeling.

"Maybe men who live those double lives don't realize what they do to women," Jacob noted.

"Well, they should. I couldn't even imagine how I would feel if I found out you were creeping with men."

Jacob snorted. "Woman, that ain't never gonna happen!"

"Well, I'm sure that's what most women think, until it happens to them. Bad enough when you have to worry about your man creeping with another woman. But a man? My God!"

Jacob sat up, giving me a fake look of shock. "So are you questioning my manhood now?"

"No, silly!" I punched his leg underneath the covers, and then moved my fingers slowly up his thigh, till they rested on the semihardness between his legs. "I don't think you have anything to worry about, when it comes to your manhood."

He moved slightly, making himself jump against my fingers. "You're the one who has nothing to worry about in that department. Trust me!"

We both laughed together. It felt so good. For some odd reason, though, my laughter turned to tears. They spilled over my brown cheeks like a dam and wouldn't stop coming. This was becoming a habit!

"What's wrong?" Jacob asked, extremely concerned.

Here, lately, he hadn't seen me cry before now. But it was a different type of crying, of tears. It was tears of relief and revelation.

"I dunno," I sputtered out. "I think I just realized how much time I've wasted, especially our time. I love you, Jacob. I have always loved you."

"You think I don't know that, Kimmy? You think I haven't known it? I've always seen who you were. You're this tough FBI agent who put on this persona to protect herself. But I saw you, I still do. You're tough, you're beautiful—"

"Oh, Jacob, please. Not!"

"Yes, you are," he remarked, bending forward and kissing my cheek. "You're also scared, needy, even though you would never admit it. And you just needed those things validated within yourself."

"You forgot the most important part," I whispered.

"What's that?"

"I am totally, completely, in love with you, Jacob White. And I always will be."

As Jacob took me into his arms and covered his lips with mine, I felt myself home, for the very first time.

And for me, "sealed with a kiss," took on a whole new meaning.

Book Club
Questions / Reader's Guide

1) Who are your favorite characters in *Kisses Aren't Always Sweet*, and why?

2) Do you think Kimberla had a valid reason to be angry and jealous when she caught Lolita at Jacob's house at midnight?

3) What is your opinion of online relationships? And do you think the situations with Catwomyn75 and her male victims were realistic?

4) Do you think the corruption that was mentioned in this story was realistic about the FBI, and could something like that really happen?

5) Do you think the bureau was wrong to keep information away from Kimberla and Jacob that could and did endanger their lives, even if it was for what they considered a good reason?

6) What did you think of Kimberla's connection issues with Jacob? And do you think she was wrong in keeping her past rape a secret from him?

7) What do you think about the growing epidemic of down low or bisexual black men?

8) Were you empathic towards Catwomyn75, once you learned the reason she was killing these men? Why or why not?

9) Do you think men really understand the seriousness of living double lives? And do you agree with some of their excuses, that what a woman doesn't know won't hurt her? Why or why not?

10) Do you agree with Kimberla and Jacob's decision to leave the bureau?

11) Would you like to read another story about the life and adventures of Kimberla Bacon and Jacob White?

A Letter To My Readers

I wanted to explain why I wrote *Kisses Aren't Always Sweet*. I wrote it to give an exciting, suspenseful tale of betrayal, pain and revenge. I didn't want to give the impression that all men are dogs or that the men in this book deserved the horrible things that happened to them. But with every choice we make, there are either good or bad consequences. Unfortunately for these men, their choices left them in dire straits.

We have an epidemic in our society today, especially in the black community that affects us all. When one talks about down low men, or straight men who sleep with men, the topic is usually the physical damage that's done to women and the rising HIV statistic that plagues them. This is usually because of the actions of black men who lie about their sexuality and behavior, or women who close their eyes to the vivid truth that is right in front of them. Rarely do you hear about the emotional impact this has on women and/or the children who are left behind. This story is about a woman who is damaged mentally and emotionally to the point where she loses herself and her humanity, and takes her hurt out on the opposite sex. There is an emotional pain from this type of betrayal that only a woman who has been there, could ever understand. It makes you question your worth as a woman, it makes you question your worth as a human being. This story is a fictional take that could someday be a reality for men who selfishly pursue an alternative lifestyle while still holding on to the women who love them.

I hope you enjoyed reading this novel as much as I enjoyed writing it. And I hope it leaves my readers with thought-provoking questions that can someday do away with this unhealthy trend that is growing in our communities.

JDaniels*